I0598764

THE GIRL
WHO SAID
GOODBYE
FOR
THE LAST TIME

A Descent into Madness

By
J. Wayne Frye

THE GIRL WHO SAID GOODBYE
FOR THE LAST TIME

The Author

Wayne Frye's Aaron Adams series has been popular among Canadian mystery lovers since first appearing in 2005. He provides satirical political commentary to many Canadian newspapers, and his books on politics have created a great deal of controversy. He has written marketing/advertising textbooks, been a successful U.S. university hockey coach, professor, university president and served as a marketing consultant to hockey teams and motion picture companies. He has been cited for his work with inner-city gang children in the Los Angeles area and been active in the anti-globalization movement. He became a Canadian citizen in 2003 and lives in Ladysmith, Vancouver Island, British Columbia and Cavite, Philippines.

Other Books by J. Wayne Frye

Hockey Mania and the Mystery of Nancy Running Elk
Something Evil in the Darkness at Hopkins House
How Hockey Saved a Jew From the Holocaust:
The Rudi Ball Story
The Catastrophic Calamities of a Village Idiot
Fighting for Justice in the Land of Hypocrisy
Guide to Alternative Education (13 Editions)
Cataclysmic Dreams in Black and White
The Girl who Stirred Up the Whirlwind
Introduction to Advertising
Fall From Apocalypse
Advertising Lab Manual
Promotions Workbook
Public Relations Workbook
Advertising Design
Armageddon Now
Worth
When Jesus Came to Jersey as the Son of Thunder
When Jesus Came to Canada to Lead an Indigenous Rebellion
Canadian Angels of Mercy – Nurses in Times of Peril
Points of Rebellion: Aboriginals Who Fought for Justice
Lynton Curls Her Hair
Lynton Buys a Cell-Phone and Hears the Voice of Doom
Chablis: Avenging Angel for the Forgotten

J. Wayne Frye

THE GIRL WHO SAID GOODBYE
FOR THE LAST TIME

TABLE OF CONTENTS

THE GIRL WHO SAID GOODBYE
FOR THE LAST TIME

TO: Joy - a woman who is the epitome of the beauty of soul that soars to the heights of understanding in a world where there is far too little compassion. One magical time she permitted me to bask in the glory of her presence as she used her cell phone to allow me to spend the day with her. It is a day I shall always treasure. She is a shiny jewel and her name bespeaks of what she brings to those lucky enough to know her – JOY.

And of course, as always, to my beloved muse, **Lynton Viñas**. Too often we underestimate the power of a touch, a smile, a kind word, a listening ear, an honest compliment, or the smallest act of caring, all of which have the potential to turn a life around.

JWF

Copyright 2014 by J. Wayne Frye

Catalogue Number: 8341-945-822

ISBN: 978-1-928183-00-6

**Fireside Books – Victoria, British Columbia
Peninsula Publishing Consortium**

THE GIRL WHO SAID GOODBYE
FOR THE LAST TIME

PROLOGUE
THE LIGHT FADED

The bright lights outside the dingy hotel room window flashed a neon beacon of lost promise for those who had finally descended to the bottom of despair on a street of broken dreams. The room was a barren pit of squandered hope, as beside Aaron Adams' bed sat the beautiful Jasmine Alexander, who had been searching for him for so long. She held the frail hand of the 82 year old man and reflected back on the day they met in the streets of Stockholm. Aaron Adams had been a vibrant 62 year old man, who impressed Jasmine as nothing more than an aging Lothario who thought he could actually pick up a 26 year old girl. However, she found him, despite all his faults, to be her saviour from, not only the infamous assassin, the *Whirlwind*, but from an existence that was more transitory searching than solid foundation. Hers was a lonely battle, and beside her stood her champion through it all. Yet, this champion had deep rooted flaws that plagued her and made her cringe with heartache as she allowed her love for Aaron to prevail through all the anguish.

Finally, after 20 years of this burden, Aaron received an envelope from Jasmine that he had not opened, but simply carried in his pocket as a reminder of what he had lost. Even though Aaron

THE GIRL WHO SAID GOODBYE
FOR THE LAST TIME

was old now, in bad health and extremely frail, he was aware of his shortcomings. For that reason, he had never opened the envelope; for fear that it would cause him more pain than he could bear. He knew what it said, but he simply could not read the words of goodbye from his beloved.

Slowly, the old, frail Aaron looked up into Jasmine's eyes and seemed to beg for forgiveness. The pleading in his eyes made her bend over and whisper in his ears, "it is OK, Aaron. I am here for you. I will never desert you in your time of need."

Aaron, in a wispy, barely audible voice replied, "I want you to be the last thing I see before the dark veil of eternity covers me. Stay by my side please, so that I may remember the most valuable thing in my life that I threw away through foolishness."

Thus began the final saga in the life of Aaron Adams, as the hotel neon sign suddenly sputtered out and the light faded.

J. Wayne Frye

THE GIRL WHO SAID GOODBYE FOR THE LAST TIME

CHAPTER 1
MY LAST THOUGHTS WILL BE OF HER

As a young girl, the precocious Jasmine Alexander had known depravation, and she was actually more of a parent than were her mother and father, whose meagre means and childlike ways made the family struggle for survival. Yet, she was strong and resolute, never succumbing to fear. Any trepidation she had was only of a passing nature, because she felt she could overcome any obstacle. Her determination, drive, desire and will made her admirable to all who knew her. Still, she was harbouring fears of her own that would never be revealed, but they preyed upon her mind and she seemed to be lost until she found her champion in Aaron Adams. Yet, her champion also had deep flaws that would tear at her heart, destroying so much and opening a pit of anguish.

Meanwhile, Aaron Adams, as a boy, was shy and clung to his mother with desperation. He always sought the warmth of her arms for deep within lay a fear of the world and his ability to cope with it. Even as a newborn, there was an aura about him that seemed to portend a coming calamity of the mind that would forever trap him in the depths of depression that would gradually overwhelm him and destroy his life. Within all men's minds there are forces at work that are never privy to those who only see the outer surface but cannot observe the turmoil that rages within.

Thus, these two people were destined to come together and spend 20 years in search of compatibility. It did occur often, but unfortunately, was only transitory in nature and lacked the genuine depth that Aaron thought was there. He never realized his fits of despair were tearing Jasmine apart inside, causing an anguish that simply could never heal. Through it all, she loved him deeply, but suffered in lonely silence his descent into despair that would be followed by periods of quiet euphoria that she hoped would signal the end of his and her mental anguish. This was a man on fire inside and the fire was not only consuming him and devouring him; it were also destroying Jasmine, making her flounder in a hopeless search for that one spark of salvation that would make her beloved champion the man he should be.

So, this is a story of two people who met on a dark Stockholm street, but it is also the story of one man's mental anguish and how the woman he loved was nearly destroyed by it. She was the real champion, not him. It was she who endured the unendurable, who nursed him through his bouts of depression, reached out with compassion when he wept as the lonely darkness of his mind that there was something wrong with him. The friends he did have and the family who cared about him simply could not erase that feeling of deep doubt that was carving a hole in his psyche.

When Aaron was about seven, he began to notice that his father often seemed displeased with him, because he could not do mechanical things very well. Once while trying to learn how to build things with an erector set, his father worked diligently to show him how to make a crane. Aaron felt a sense of accomplishment when he completed the task, which was actually mostly done by his father. Then, his father disassembled the crane and told Aaron to build it again. Aaron struggled desperately to build it, but each step he took was wrong. His father was patient for awhile, but finally lost his patience and blurted out, "forget it son, you're too stupid to learn."

The hurt felt by Aaron was not physically present, but it was the first time that his little mind would hear those words from his father. It would not be the last. Over the years, the words "you're stupid" or "you're weak minded" would be hurled at him from his father like a knife thrust through the heart of an animal being gutted for the spit. Just as Judy had told him that he was not worthy with her "yuck," now his own father saw him as useless, worthless and unable to measure up to the standards set for normal people. That was it. Yes,

THE GIRL WHO SAID GOODBYE
FOR THE LAST TIME

Aaron looked deep within himself at the age of seven and decided that he was truly an unworthy human being whose existence was nothing more than a lonely struggle to survive in a world where he was not wanted. This world would often close in on Aaron and cloister him in despair.

Aaron's father was a chronic alcoholic who provided well for his family. Yet, there never seemed to be enough time for Aaron. He could always find time to drink with friends, but when Aaron wanted to play ball or just pal around, his father would say, "can't do that son. Have to work and earn money. You will never get anywhere in life sitting in a movie, watching television or playing ball. Learn skills that will make you a value in the workplace. You can never start too young."

Money seemed to be at the core of his father's thinking, which was somewhat understandable since he had survived the Great Depression, which had wrecked havoc all across America. Still, little Aaron could not understand the need for money when all he wanted was time and a few kind words from his father.

The pain felt by those who suffer mental illness cannot be described in mere words. It is beyond the comprehension of those who do not suffer the agony of desperation that makes the afflicted always on the edge of a cliff, teetering precariously, trying to keep from falling into the abyss.

When Aaron was eight years old, he went to the car races with his dad and two uncles. On the way back, as Aaron sat in the back seat the three men passed around a bottle of whiskey. Aaron was used to whiskey being almost an every day part of his life, so there seemed nothing particularly unusual about it. As they slowly approached a large rock that had fallen onto the road, Aaron instinctively said to his father, who was driving, "better stop daddy, there's a rock in the road."

His father replied, "I stop for nothing son. A man who stops never will get anywhere in life. Always keep moving forward. Weak thinking will get you nowhere."

Again, Aaron went over in his mind those words he had heard as he sat on the living room floor trying to build a crane with his erector set. Yes, Aaron was weak-minded, because the man he admired most in the world said he was. It had to be true.

The seeds of self-doubt are planted at an early age. Much of Aaron's doubt about himself actually flowed from the words of a man who, himself, had great doubts. The mental problems that affected Aaron all his life had also afflicted his father, who self-medicated his depression through the consumption of copious amounts of alcohol. Aaron would never take a drink of alcohol during his lifetime, but he got drunk in another way. He medicated himself by withdrawing and hiding from a world that seemed to overwhelm him. No matter what his age, he was always that little frightened boy who wanted the warmth of his mother's arms to protect him from the harmful elements that seemed to be all around him. There were demons in his mind, but he also saw demons that lurked about in search of him, trying to coax him into a world inhabited by those who judged him as inferior and unworthy. He was always frightened, always on guard, always wary of what awaited him down the corridor, in the next room, under his bed, behind the tree or just over the hill. He faced each day with great trepidation and the expectation that he would once again be rejected because he was weak minded and unworthy. Each day was agony as he awakened and prepared his own breakfast, because his mother was too tired to get up. She was exhausted every morning, because she would have to spend the evenings going from one drinking establishment to another with a husband who was as much a child as Aaron was. Aaron did not blame her, because he understood that if she did not go there would be a heated argument with a man who would have no other way than his way.

THE GIRL WHO SAID GOODBYE
FOR THE LAST TIME

His father was a man capable of deep compassion, but he also had a raging storm within him that could lead to vindictive cruelty that made many shiver in fear of what impending calamity might be wrought by a man who far too often seemed to lose physical and mental control.

Often, little Aaron would witness violent fits of anger that, even at eight years old, made his little mind wonder if he, too, would suffer the same tirades of anger that gripped his father in a labyrinth from which there appeared no escape.

Many traumatic incidents in childhood leave a deep impression on the mind that will simply never heal with time. No matter what age, those incidents invariably bring out fears that may be suppressed for years, but they will always be there. One can never underestimate the effect one solitary event, no matter how brief can have on a life. The effect can be positive or negative or both. It can be conscious or subconscious. What seems inconsequential at the time, can be so profound in the long run that it bores its way deep into the recesses of the mind to trap us in psychological chains that we are often unaware exist.

Once, a famous writer, who had just turned 80, recalled an incident as he and a friend waited on the dock for his sister to arrive in New York on the Queen Mary. He said to his friend, "When I

THE GIRL WHO SAID GOODBYE
FOR THE LAST TIME

was a 20, I was awaiting the arrival of a ship right here on this same dock with my mother and father on it. I waved wildly as I saw them on the deck. As the passengers descended down the gangplank, I caught sight of a young lady dressed in white satin with a brocade black hat on that was slightly tilted to one side. I looked upon the most angelic face I had ever seen. There was a glow to it, and a countenance that seemed to be saying "this is the angel of light." My heart raced and I leaned over the railing, trying to see her as she disappeared into the throng gathering around the gangplank. That incident lasted no more than five seconds. Yet, there has not been a day of my life since then that I have not thought of that woman. My wonderful wife, my three magnificent children could not erase her from my heart. Those five seconds have left an empty spot in my soul, as I wonder what it would have been like to be with her for a brief time, to hear her soft melodic voice, gaze at her sheepish laugh and absorb the beauty of what was obviously a coy nature. I am an old man who is nearing death now, and although I only gazed upon her for five seconds, I know that when the veil of darkness passes over me, my last thoughts will be of her."

J. Wayne Frye

THE GIRL WHO SAID GOODBYE
FOR THE LAST TIME

CHAPTER 2
YOU AIN'T NEVER DONE NOTHING

For little Aaron, who was tall but frail as a child, his salvation in a life seething with turmoil at home was his beloved grandmother who always had kind words of encouragement for him. Had it not been for her, the anguish that penetrated his little heart would have been too much to bear. It was she who lifted him up when he was down, soothed his hurt with warm arms and whispered softly to him "everything will be alright, grandmother is here." And she always was until Aaron turned 22 and was awaiting his impending induction into the army. A stroke felled his beloved grandmother and as he kneeled beside her bed, pleading with the unconscious woman not to die, the last string that held his tortured soul together was slowly unravelling.

Upon her death, Aaron paid a visit to a jeweller and purchased a small locket engraved with the words "I will love you forever, Aaron" that he placed around her neck as she lay in the coffin. So strong was his belief in their love for one another that he actually thought that she would come from the beyond and return the necklace as a sign that she was still with him. For years, he looked in various places, hoping that she would send him that message of love. His tortured mind needed her as his foundation to survive in a world that kept overwhelming him at every turn. She died in May, and as he awaited his July induction into the army, the trepidation and psychological fear often overwhelmed him as he sat in lonely silence in his room at his mother and father's house. He gazed up at the ceiling, tracing designs of battlefields in his mind, as he anticipated he would be shipped to Vietnam to save another country for democracy. This was the first time that he began to explore the true meaning of democracy and ask himself if that was what America had? The poverty, the callousness, the corporate control, the constant military intervention did not seem the way to spread democracy. Rather, it appeared the way to sow the seeds of fear to keep people in bondage to something that was more a figment of the gullible public's imagination than reality.

So distraught over the loss of his grandmother, he turned to his girlfriend for solace, and to her credit, she gave it to him with all her heart. Brandy Helman was still in university, with one year left before she would receive her teaching degree. Aaron had never suggested marriage, even though he had given her an engagement ring, but in the back of his warped, sick mind he developed a plan to replace his grandmother with another woman who would offer him the love he so sorely needed. Although callous in one respect, in another, it offered him hope that there was still a way to find someone besides his grandmother to love him. His inner turmoil and need for love had fostered a decision not of the heart but of his warped mind. Thus, the marriage, from the very beginning, was not based on love. It was predicated upon the practicality of making Aaron's life better in the army with a wife. This would be one of Aaron's biggest mistakes, because the two of them were completely incompatible and many years of turmoil, pain and acrimony would follow. Neither of them was a saint in the marriage, but Aaron's disease would eventually tear everything asunder and the marriage would end with bitterness and hatred from a wife who, though certainly not very agreeable herself, suffered despair as a result of a man who was sick in mind and spirit. It was during this time that Aaron had manifested the first signs of mood swings that would eventually destroy his life. Only Aaron's body was spared from the demons that tortured him, and eventually, that too, would suffer and wither into a shell of hopelessness.

Incidents from childhood are seared into our minds like a brand is burned onto cattle. Hair will not grow over the brand as it goes deep into the flesh. The same applied to Aaron's state of mind that had been seared with a hot iron of despair by so many incidents that made him feel inferior. He desperately covered it up through outward manifestations of gregariousness. Yet, always within was that demon that tore at his insides.

THE GIRL WHO SAID GOODBYE
FOR THE LAST TIME

There are many forms of pain. It is much easier to treat a wound on the arm, foot or abdomen, but the pain of the mind can not be cleansed with iodine and a bandage. That pain spreads like a raging cancer gobbling up all the good that exists and allowing the evil to spread and grow. Although it can be arrested and held at bay for awhile, eventually, it finds an opening and releases its fury, causing mayhem and turmoil of the foulest kind. This was the lonely battle Aaron had fought all his life, and he would die still fighting it.

During Aaron's early struggles, Jasmine had not even been born, but in 1963, on the day she entered the world of sorrow that had already engulfed Aaron, the sun, no doubt, gave off a special twinkle, signifying the arrival of an angel who would walk the earth reaching out with kindness and compassion to all who crossed her path. She was vintage wine that had cooled and long aged in the deep-delved earth. Jasmine was dance, song and sunburnt mirth. The bubbles of hope beaded with effervescence, reaching to the brim with the gaiety of a world filled with possibilities rather than hopelessness. But for Aaron, the world was filled with demons of darkness that penetrated his mind and soul as he tried to deal with that inner turmoil that was raging all about. The demons were trying desperately to claim him for their own, and he felt powerless in the titanic struggle that whirled within.

Jasmine was not like the normal girl. Although shy, she gradually became the person on whom her mother, father and sister relied. She was the one who could fix a broken faucet, patch a hole in the wall, paint the wooden siding of the house, gather vegetables from the tiny garden and read instruction manuals to put things together. Barely six years old, her parents relied on her knowledge to help them solve problems. Where Aaron had wallowed in self-doubt, Jasmine developed an aura of invincibility and truly believed that there was nothing she could not accomplish.

Growing up poor is an affliction that far too many people in the world must face. In places like America, poverty is almost glorified as a breeding ground for character building in the great land of opportunity, but that opportunity is only reserved for the few at the expense of the many. Jasmine was not born into privilege, but with determination and drive, she was going to claw her way out of the abject poverty that surrounded her. She saw life as an opportunity to grow and prosper, while Aaron saw life as a burden foisted on him by two parents who decided to fornicate one night and bring him into a world he loathed and wished would simply go away. He often would lie in bed and cover his head with the sheet, only leaving a small hole to breathe out of. That was his way of escaping into a cocoon of safety that protected him from the world.

Many people are prisoners of despair, often caused by chemical imbalances in the brain. Aaron was one of those people. Add to that, a home where turmoil reigns supreme and an alcoholic father who keeps reminding you how useless you are and the depths of despair to which one can sink are unfathomable. Aaron was destined to live this life as long as his father was alive, because even as an adult, he would often hear that he was weak-minded. Even the death of his father would never erase from Aaron's mind the words his father once uttered to him when he was visiting with his new wife, the lovely Jasmine Alexander. Those words that would continue to ring deep within Aaron's tormented mind several times each day of his life: "you ain't never done nothing and you never will. You ain't never done nothing and you never will."

THE GIRL WHO SAID GOODBYE
FOR THE LAST TIME

CHAPTER 3
THE STORMY SEAS OF THE MIND

Aaron looked around at the soiled linen on the bed where his frail body lay. It was torn and ragged. The room seemed to be swirling. He glanced over at the hotel sign that was bracketed to the brick wall outside his half-opened window. His beloved Jasmine had returned to his side, holding his hand and looking down upon him with the compassion of an angel from heaven. Breathing rhythmically, his chest rising up and down exposing his bones where the aging flesh had seemingly melted away into a leathery pulp, he recalled that old George Jones song *He Stopped Loving Her Today*.

Aaron had told Jasmine on the third or fourth date that he would love her until the day he died. He sensed that she had found someone else to fill the void Aaron had put into her aching heart. Why wouldn't she? The time went slowly by, but her memory always preyed upon his mind. He kept her many pictures hanging on the walls of the dingy hotel room that he called home. He paced the floor in solitude going over all the wrongs he had committed, and yet, she had loved him through it all, until she finally put that note in the envelope. She had given him his last chance and walked out of his life for good. Realizing his mistakes, it was now simply too late. She was gone. Still, like the George Jones song, he could only stop loving her when they carried him away.

The pain of the mind is as real as a wound from a sharp instrument penetrating the flesh. This pain is a seed that grows into a bush of thorns that prick the senses and cuts deep into the heart of a man. Aaron had dealt with this all his life, and as he lay on the bed feeling the warmth of Jasmine's touch, he began to reflect on a life of mental anguish and self-doubt, a life of lonely, quiet desperation that had made him a prisoner of anguish. His blurry vision made the room seem to be in a fog, and as he gazed up at the water-stained, filthy ceiling the past cascaded through his mind like the gentle flow of a crystal clear stream bubbling over smooth rocks.

Aaron, as a child, had always been fascinated by detective shows on television. He dreamed of being a private detective like his heroes who were self-assured, suave and exhibited a smooth savoir faire that made the ladies swoon with delight when around them. His was often a fantasy world where he was everything in his mind that he knew he could never be in the reality of the world that so often overwhelmed him. The torment and wretchedness of his existence made him desperate on the inside, but his exterior was masked with a determination and self-assuredness that made everyone marvel at his finesse and uncanny ability to master the art of communication. From the CEO to the janitor in his office building, people looked at Aaron as a man who exuded self-confidence. His charming sense of humour hid the distress and torment that raged within. There was hardly a day that he did not make his lonely journey into the depths of despair. No matter how hard he fought against the raging storm within, the torment and agony would always eventually win out over the contentment and happiness he so desperately sought.

In high school, Aaron hid his affliction of the mind by jocularity and clownishness that made his classmates think that he possessed a great appetite and passion for life. However, underneath was nothing but fear of life. Each morning, as he prepared to leave for school, he would look around at the familiar objects that made up what was more a house than a home, because a home was a place of peace and tranquility, but that did not exist for Aaron. His house was always filled with people drinking into the wee hours of the morning as he desperately tried to get some sleep or study for a test. There were often fits of rage from a father who, himself, was most likely suffering from the same malady that afflicted Aaron. Aaron had no medication to help him cope, but his father coped through self-medication with alcohol. As Aaron aged, he could see that the addiction to alcohol was consuming the man he admired most, and it was causing intense suffering for him, his mother and young sister. He vowed to never let alcohol touch his lips, as he had an intense fear that it would consume his body and soul, destroying those he loved in the process.

Always alone in the morning, because his mother was too exhausted to crawl out of bed and fix breakfast after a only a few hours sleep, Aaron felt a sense of dread that he would have to spend another day hiding his pain, hiding the truth of the agony that raged within him. It was a daily battle that exhausted his young mind as he continued the charade of happiness. Aaron was not really living; he only existed.

At the age of 16, Aaron was attending a convention for student council members in nearby Raleigh. While standing in a line to enter the auditorium, he desperately wanted to talk to a girl behind him. Now Aaron had been on a few dates, but his fear of not being appealing had always kept him leery of the opposite sex. He found that around girls he would always get dryness in his mouth and his heart would beat a little faster. The early childhood rejection by Judy had never faded into the reassesses of his mind; consequently, he was always timid when talking to girls and extremely awkward in his approach. Yet, as he looked at the statuesque girl with dark hair standing behind him, he desperately searched for words to motivate her interest. They simply would not come, but fortunately, it was she who opened up the conversation.

"Don't you just hate having to stand in line for everything? That is what I hate most about school, the damn lines."

Aaron, nervous, but now feeling more confident, replied, "Yeah, the only line I like is the one that forms to get out the school door when the final bell rings. By the way, my name is Aaron."

Smiling, she said, "I am Penny, pleased to meet you Aaron."

Fortunately, the girl was from a city near Aaron's hometown. He was delighted to know that and as they continued the conversation, Aaron, who had experienced some fondling and masturbatory play with a few girls, was shocked at how open the young lady was about sex. It became evident to him when she commented on the short skirt worn by another girl in the line with the rather risqué comment, "If girl's skirts get any shorter, they are going to have to brush more than the hair on their heads."

Aaron was immediately infatuated by her frankness about sex, and he felt that customary tingle between his legs and the erection that often caused him embarrassment around girls. Penny looked at him and said, "If you ask me for a date, I might be able to take care of that problem you're having."

Thus began what was to be Aaron's first serious love affair. On the first date they played miniature golf, had a desert at Hot Shoppe, cruised the local drive-in restaurant and finished the evening off by intense passionate kissing in the car while Penny, with her hand, took care of that problem Aaron always had around girls. Before long, Penny grew tired of using her hands and they progressed to intercourse, which became more intense over time.

The budding romance kept Aaron's agony of the mind at bay for a while, but those old doubts about himself began to play out in different ways. Fearful of losing her, he became possessive and wanted to know what she was doing all the time. She was also an avid smoker, which Aaron found distasteful and un-lady like. Insisting that she stop smoking, he became obsessed with helping her quit a habit that he thought was no different than his father' addiction to alcohol. Aaron knew that nicotine was nothing more than a drug that caused temporary euphoria. Having fallen deeply in love with a boy she found kind, caring and generous, Penny tried hard to stop smoking, but when she was away from Aaron, she would often slip a cigarette.

THE GIRL WHO SAID GOODBYE
FOR THE LAST TIME

Now, at the time, it was a much different world when it came to smoking than it is today, so most high schools in North Carolina, which was the home of the tobacco industry, allowed smoking by students on campus. Aaron, always adapt at playing private eye, decided one day that he was going to check up on Penny and see if she was slipping cigarettes. He cut school that day and knowing where she always parked in the school parking lot in Greensboro, which was only 30 minutes from Aaron's home, he hid behind a large oak tree as she walked out to her car with some other girls puffing away on a cigarette. In Aaron's warped mind, he felt she was cheating on him. It was no different than being with another boy.

That night, Aaron confronted her and it was the first of many arguments they would have over the coming weeks and months, not just over her smoking, but about everything from the length of her skirts to the number of times she was brushing her teeth each and every day. Despite his outward appearance of extreme happiness, Aaron was manufacturing in his mind reasons that she did not love him, and, in fact, his actions were beginning to drive a wedge between them. So fragile was his mind that each little slight made him fearful that he was losing her.

Aaron's father, who allowed him to drive the family station wagon, noticed that Aaron always had a thick blanket in the back of the car. He jokingly said one day, "Nothing like a station wagon for dates, uh son?"

Aaron, somewhat embarrassed, replied, "Yeah, when Penny and I go to the drive-in, she sometimes gets cold."

His father said, "Well, while you are keeping her warm, make sure you use protection. You're too young to be a father."

From that point on, Aaron and his father became more open with one another. His father even offered to buy condoms for him, but Aaron and Penny had gone beyond that stage. In fact, they had never used them. Of course, he lied to his father and said he had plenty. In fact, he even started carrying one in his wallet just in case his father asked about it again.

This laissez-faire attitude about their sexual relationship was about to have dire consequences for the two young people. Aaron, the first few times having sex always pulled out of her before ejaculation, foolishly thinking that would avert pregnancy. However, as men are prone to do, when encouraged by a woman's passionate pleas to let them feel their seed inside them, Aaron fell prey to passion rather than common sense. Over a period of months he planted his seed in her almost daily, as she pleaded for him to unload his love into her body.

Their favourite parking spot in Greensboro was an old rock quarry just outside of town. Aaron would lower the rear seats, spread out the blanket and make the station wagon a lovemaking nest of wild fornication. For Aaron and Penny, the difference between love and lust was blurred.

One night in late February, as they sat in the front seat after a few hours of frantic lovemaking in the back of the station wagon, Penny just casually mentioned to Aaron that her period was two weeks overdue.

Aaron, intending to attend university the following fall, was shocked that all his plans of studying criminology and finally becoming the private detective who would be involved in mystery and intrigue seemed to be evaporating. He was in deep trouble and racing through his mind was a kaleidoscope of mayhem as he saw nothing in his future but toil in a dead end job, because he had been so foolish. Now, he would have to go to work rather than university because he would soon have a wife and child to support. That dark veil of fear was closing in on him, and there seemed no way out. This was 1960's, and in America, the only thing as powerful as a corporation was the church. Abortion was illegal thanks to the influence of religion. So, foolish young people's lives were ruined day in and day out, because a woman's body was not hers to control.

While Aaron was frantic with trepidation, Penny was euphoric and already planning for a wedding in the near future. She was in love with Aaron. In flash of reality, Aaron realized that he had never been in love with Penny, only in lust. What could he do?

Aaron went home that night and as he lay in bed, he went over his options. He knew that abortion, although illegal, was obtainable if you knew the right person. They were performed all the time in dank, dark corners of a world where illegalities were ignored for profit. He had the money, as he had been working for almost two years, but he had two obstacles to overcome. First, Penny wanted to marry him and probably would refuse to have an abortion. Then, if he could get her to agree to one, he had to locate the person to perform it. To an individual who already was dealing with the inner turmoil of the mind, this burden had Aaron teetering on a precipice with a dark pit of hopelessness below waiting to devour him.

Who could he turn to in his time of need? His grandmother was always a source of compassion, but he could not tell her about it out of shame. Then, there was his father, often a compassionate man, but also the man who constantly told him how dumb he was. Yeah, thought Aaron, I am really proving it now.

Another two weeks dragged on and Aaron, despite his consternation, like most young men, still found the energy to fornicate. He had no fear of impregnating Penny now. The sex was still great, but day after day, Aaron struggled with what he was going to do. Each day that passed was another day closer to the deadline for a safe abortion. He mentioned to Penny that without an education, he would not be able to support her and the baby the way he wanted. Slowly, Penny began to realize that they were both too young to be parents. They were barely out of adolescence.

One night as they sat in the quarry talking after extremely passionate sex, Penny said, "Aaron, you get someone who can do it safely and I will get an abortion.

A great weight was lifted from Aaron's psyche. He might be able to salvage his future, but there was still the problem of finding someone to perform the procedure. No doctor would do it, because performing abortions was tantamount to murder at the time. The lack of safe, legal abortions drove women to back alley practitioners who often botched the job, sometimes even causing the death of the woman. This was a tenuous situation that required a more mature and level headed person than Aaron.

Aaron was never fearful of physical abuse from his father, but his verbal abuse could often reduce the now 17 year old Aaron to quiet tears that he would often shed in the privacy of his bedroom. He always tried to avoid crying in front of his father, because his father saw that as a sign of weakness. However, his father was a man who knew how to solve problems like no other man Aaron knew. People were always coming to him for help, and Aaron was desperate. He would have to swallow his pride and tell his father about the dilemma he was in as a result of stupidity. Again, in Aaron's fragile mental state, he was once again proving his father right. He was weak minded and unable to be a real man.

His father ran an incredibly successful business and was always working late, often sitting around his downtown office and drinking with employees and friends. Fortunately for misery-afflicted Aaron, he was alone when Aaron walked in and said, "Daddy, I really need to talk to you about something important."

Aaron sat down, lowered his head and started crying. As was customary, his father said, "You never solve anything by crying son. Dry your eyes and tell me the problem."

THE GIRL WHO SAID GOODBYE
FOR THE LAST TIME

Still snivelling, Aaron said, "I got Penny pregnant."

Letting out a sigh, his father replied, "Well, that is a pretty big problem, but one that can be solved."

For the first time in his adolescence, Aaron looked at his father and felt loved. Never before had he sensed love from this man who was tough and aloof with his emotions. Although still unemotional, his father lifted Aaron's spirits as he felt that he had a champion among men on his side.

His father asked if Penny was willing to get an abortion. Aaron, now a bit less emotional, said, "I think so daddy. I believe she will."

"Then you have no problem son. There is a woman in Durham who will take care of this in a few minutes. Make sure Penny is willing, and I will give you the $300 and you can take her there in a couple of days."

Religion is like a disease in America. It spreads as much evil as good. The moral guardians of virtue want to control people's thoughts and deeds. The young are indoctrinated to believe that not following the path outlined in the Bible will condemn an individual to languish in the burning fires of hell where a red devil is running around with a pitchfork to prod you forward into the hot fires of damnation. Young, impressionable minds easily accept this nightmarish tactic and form their beliefs based on fear, not fact.

Although neither were church goers, Aaron and Penny were victims of this fear tactic, That sinfulness seed had been planted when they were young and attending Sunday school, which made them feel as if they were committing a mortal sin. Aaron lay in his room at night, staring at the ceiling and prayed to a God, in whom he did not believe, to please forgive him for this sin.

Three nights before Penny's scheduled appointment to terminate the pregnancy, Aaron received a call from her around 8:00 PM. Penny, very excitingly, said, "I miscarried. It was twins."

Aaron felt like he had been saved from the fires of hell, although the thought of losing those two children would prey upon his mind the rest of his life. His future was secure once again, and from that day forward, he always carried condoms in his wallet, not to impress his father, but to avoid ever committing such a stupid act again.

Eventually, Penny and Aaron drifted apart as many lovers do. While in university, Aaron diligently devoted himself to his studies and his mood swings and bouts with depression seemed to subside a bit, as he really enjoyed the camaraderie with his fellow students and even felt more secure and confident, but those old feelings of inferiority and being out of place in a world he did not understand still wreaked havoc on his psyche from time to time.

Although he was relatively popular, still, in his mind he felt inferior to everyone with whom he associated. Often called one of the smartest students in school, it had little effect on his self-esteem, because he knew that deep within he was not smart and that he was majoring in a subject that was relatively easy. He was just a grand manipulator who had learned how to fool people into thinking he was smart. In his mind, he knew he was living a lie.

Dormitory living makes the communal common, and Aaron, although friendly, still felt that he lacked the ability to really fit in with those around him. It was in university that he began to experience mood swings, where one minute he would be euphoric and the next he would sink into a morass of despair. Of course, he did not recognize them as such, simply passing them off as part of his feelings of inferiority. Having a roommate made it impossible for Aaron to crawl into his shell and hide from the world in lonely contemplation as often as he would have liked. It was a time of discovery for Aaron, but the one thing he needed to discover – the sickness of his mind, eluded him.

Aaron, despite his relative popularity, continued to suffer from mood swings that veered between emotional highs and euphoria to deep depression. His lonely battle kept him from enjoying many of the things that make university fun. He wanted to be an active participant in events and gatherings, but always, in the back of his mind, he felt that he was not like other people. He was not worthy of love and affection. Consequently, he often retreated to the safety of his room and would lie in bed simply staring at the ceiling, wondering why life was so difficult for him. Many times, when friends would come by to see him, he would ignore the knock on the door, because he simply felt too low in spirit to commune with anyone. Yet, strolling through campus, he exuded self-confidence and a gregarious nature while hiding his emotional and psychological turmoil that was wracking his mind with self-doubt and loathing. Despite all the people around him, he felt an intense loneliness, like he was cast adrift on a small boat in a raging, stormy sea of turmoil.

The mind and the body are not separate. They are entwined. When the one suffers, the other may suffer as well. Aaron was always thin, but he began to eat only once a day, and slowly his body started to react to what was happening in his mind. Desperate to put on some weight, he visited a health food store and bought a product called *Super Weight On*. The normal dosage was three tablespoons of the elixir a day. Thinking if three would put on some weight, Aaron decided that double that amount should work even better. For Aaron, whose thinness bothered him, it was just a desperate effort to curry favour with the opposite sex by making himself more physically appealing. In his mind, the body he had was abhorrent and unappealing. In order to fill out his clothes better, rather than underwear, he started wearing swim trunks, which seemed to give him more bulk. After a few months of *Super Weight On*, Aaron gave up and tried to accept that he would just have to settle for being thin. Yes, it was just another example of how he was less than suitable as a person.

A philosopher once said that the sublime is the dominion of the mind over the body that for a time can make flesh and nerve impregnable, and string the sinews like steel, so that the weak become mighty. For Aaron, there were brief times when he felt mighty and strong, ready to conquer the world. His prowess with words made him a darling of the English and Communications Departments, and a sought after speaker for various events. This should have brought him great joy, and it did at times. However, it was only transitory; because he always felt that he was just acting, not being his real self. Maybe people could like the actor, but it was too exhausting to act all the time.

There is a reciprocal relation between mental states and bodily conditions, acting both for good and ill. The good often outweighed the ill in Aaron's mind, but no matter how euphoric he got, he would always slip back into despair. He simply refused to let happiness win out over sorrow. A very wise physician once said that "every illness has two parts: what it is, and what the person thinks it is." What Aaron thought about himself was often more important and more troublesome. What he thought of life, what life meant to him was of the greatest importance and it became the bar that shut out all real health and happiness. It would take a seminal event many years later in his life for him to realize that giving into despair by lashing out at another person was a high price to pay for refusing to face the reality of his own fallibility.

Aaron was such a good student that he managed to finish a four year course in two and one-half years. Of course, rather than considering it an accomplishment, he looked upon it as stupid, because now he had no student deferment and with young men being drafted because of the Vietnam War, he had just made himself available to serve in a cause he considered nothing but

THE GIRL WHO SAID GOODBYE
FOR THE LAST TIME

foolish ill-advised empire building by America. Why should he be fighting communists? What had they ever done to him or America? What gave America the right to decide what type of economic system would prevail in another country?

So now, the stage was set for a chapter in Aaron's life that would lead to an ill-advised marriage and a job in the army that would make him a killer.

THE GIRL WHO SAID GOODBYE
FOR THE LAST TIME

CHAPTER 4
AS HIS LIFE EBBED AWAY

As alluded to in an earlier chapter, Aaron sought solace from the death of his grandmother in the arms of Brandy Helman. They planned to marry the following fall before he assumed he would be shipped off to Vietnam to protect America from the communist hordes of evil doers out to destroy capitalism. He went to Fort Bragg, North Carolina for basic training where he felt ill at ease being in a dormitory with forty other young men who all seemed more physically fit than he was. It actually gave him some comfort as he heard a few of the young men whimpering during the night. One boy was even crying for his mommy. It is difficult to describe the terror felt not only by Aaron, but by most of the young men, most under 20, who were away from home for the first time and about to be taught the art of killing.

Aaron, like all of America's youths, had been fed a steady diet of propaganda aggrandizing the USA as a beacon of freedom destined to save the world for democracy. The daily recitations of the Pledge of Allegiance with hand over the heart, the saluting of the flag and the constant attacks on the evils of communism had prepared the impressionable youths to believe they were defending freedom, when, in fact, they were defending a system of economic servitude that

J. Wayne Frye

would enslave the entire world to corporations. The army was the beginning of Aaron's questioning of the righteousness of America. Faced with the realities of war was much different than playing games with toy guns in your backyard.

The rigorous training was taxing for the slightly built Aaron, and he often lagged behind some of the others, which solidified in his mind that he was inadequate as a man. Still, he struggled valiantly to prove himself. However, one night in the barracks, a brawny 19 year old came up to Aaron and said, "You are goldbricking your way through basic training, and I am going to kick your ass."

Aaron had been in only one fight his entire life and he lost it handily. Still, as others looked on at Aaron and his challenger, he knew if he backed down he would suffer humiliation. Throwing caution to the wind, Aaron turned his back to the young man, bent over and jutted out his butt and said, "OK, there it is. Kick away!"

The entire throng of young men in the barracks burst out with laughter, including the young man who had challenged Aaron. The threat of violence had been avoided through Aaron's ability to think rather than use force. He would often use levity to disarm those who tried to engage him in violent confrontations.

THE GIRL WHO SAID GOODBYE
FOR THE LAST TIME

That night as Aaron lay in his bunk, he reflected on his mental struggles with feelings of inadequacy. Why had he not had the courage to simply fight the young man even though he had actually bested him with his levity? In Aaron's fragile mind, he had failed again, come up short as a man.

The night that his platoon had to go through what was called the infiltration course with live ammunition being fired overhead and mortar rounds going off all around them, Aaron was nervous, but it made him feel better when he saw that others were just as frightened as he was. This would show them all what a real battle was like.

There before the 400 or so soldiers was a dirt field with barbed wire strung across it about two feet above the ground. Sandbags were piled up where explosions would be set-off. Each soldier was warned that the live ammunition being fired was only four feet above the ground, so anyone standing up would be felled by the machine gun fire. The length of the course was 1500 metres. Aaron's mind was filled with a kaleidoscope of scenarios where somehow he would stand up and get mowed down by the machine gun fire. Fear had him in its grip as it did most of the others, but Aaron was already fragile mentally, so it was extremely difficult for him when the sergeant blew the whistle and they all dropped to the ground and started crawling under the barbed wire on their backs with their rifles across their chests.

Aaron had experienced nothing like this in his life. He got a rifle for his 12th birthday, but after shooting a blue-jay, he put the rifle back in its case and never fired it again. If this was war, Aaron wanted no part of it. Yet, he was determined to make it through the infiltration course. He was not going to let fear defeat him. He was fragile of mind and often of body, but he did more often than not figure out a way to get through adversity.

Realizing that standing up would bring certain death, in the darkness of the night Aaron looked skyward and was sure he was staring at the angel of death hovering overhead. As mortar rounds penetrated his eardrums and flakes of dirt and sand flew all about, Aaron tried desperately to keep calm. Still, he saw death looking down at him. The intense humid summer heat became a chill. His heart skipped with fright as he blinked his eyes trying to get the dirt out. Glancing to his left and right, he saw others struggling to work their way under the barbed wire He felt a heavy weight on his chest, as if someone had placed an anvil there. He thought about all the movies he had seen and how fast combat was. Yet, the reality was that everything seemed to be in slow motion. It was a plodding process that moved along at a snail's pace.

THE GIRL WHO SAID GOODBYE
FOR THE LAST TIME

As fatigue sat in, Aaron realized he was not even half-way to his objective. Breathing heavily, he manoeuvred under the barb wire skilfully, but caught his shirt on the wire and tore it as he proceeded forward on his back, while mortar rounds reverberated through the humid night air. This was to be the longest night of his life and all he could think about was that this was only play. In the real thing, body parts would be hurtling through the air and the screams of wounded men would be heard all about. Aaron thought back on the glorification of war in the movies and realized there was no glory in it at all. There was only pain, heartache and death.

Aaron reflected on the many times he had visited Civil War battlefields and saw the places as shrines to bravery and fidelity to duty. This night he realized they were merely shrines to stupidity. The thought crossed his mind that he might flee to Canada like other soldiers had in order to avoid going to Vietnam. No, he couldn't do that because it would disgrace his mother and father. He would have to do his duty, no matter how distasteful. He crawled forward.

Getting ever closer to his objective, Aaron recalled the final lines of a poem he once read: *let the curtain fall, and universal darkness buries all!* Yes, this was darkness of the foulest kind – the darkness of death and destruction wrought by a nation that knew no limits to its quest for control of the entire world. For the first time, he began to realize that much of what he had been told were lies. There was no glory in war! Again he recalled the last lines of a poem: *that country speeds to an untoward fate, where men are trivial and gold is great.* There were corporations making money off war and poor saps like Aaron were nothing but cannon fodder for the captains of industry.

After that night, you could see the fear etched on the faces of the young soldiers. They had all changed overnight. Now they had a different perspective on war. Gone was the swagger and bravado that had been so evident with many of the young men. It had been replaced with fear of the coming calamity, fear that death awaited in the rice paddies of Vietnam.

After basic training, Aaron was posted to Fort Leonard Wood, Missouri, where he was trained to be an intelligence analyst. The fragile mind of young Aaron was now going to become a machine of destruction for the U.S. government. This was the beginning of a long nightmare that would never end in his mind, because he would be haunted until his dying days by what he had done in the army.

At first Aaron was delighted when he received news that he was being posted to the Pentagon, since he had avoided Vietnam, but after a few days he realized just what his job was, and then his psyche took a hit and his fragile state of mind made him collapse on the sofa of his apartment in tears at the end of each day. He was analyzing intelligence gathered by a variety of agents and identifying certain individuals in villages, towns and cities in Vietnam for assassination or interrogation by the Vietnamese government that would, no doubt, use torture to extract information. Each day he agonized over what he was being forced to do and his mind was gradually unravelling with despair. He was already depressed, having gotten married in the fall to a woman whom he immediately realized was incompatible with him. She was still in university in the Midwest, but she soon joined him and the acrimony between the two started almost instantly and would continue unabated for many years.

Each day Aaron tried to figure out ways to avoid targeting individuals for assassination or interrogation. He often fabricated information that exonerated individuals, but he could not do it for everyone. He purposefully targeted older individuals with the justification in his mind that at least they had lived most of their lives. Each night he sat alone in his apartment unable to share anything with his wife, who had joined him by the summer of 1968, because he was sworn to secrecy. Then, he was sent to Vietnam for a month where he spent time in Saigon interrogating four prisoners who had vital information on the schedules of convoys on the Ho Chi Minh Trail.

He could not even tell his own wife that he was in Saigon. Supposedly he was on continuous duty assignment in the Pentagon's war room. Each day he noticed welts and bruises on the prisoners and knew that they were being tortured during interrogation. He reported it to his superiors, but their response was "they are prisoners in the custody of the Vietnamese government. All we are doing is follow-up interrogation. We are in no position to tell them how to treat their prisoners. Just do your job and get as much information as possible out of them."

The fifth day in Saigon Major Donnelley knocked on Aaron's motel room door. Aaron, lying on the bed just staring at the ceiling fan as it cut through the humid stale air, did not want to answer, because he felt the knock was a signal of impending doom. He just lay there; ignoring the incessant knocking, until the sound reverberated through his head, making him feel like his brain was exploding. The major shouted, "Adams, get your ass up. We have a field assignment."

They did not call Aaron's unit in the Pentagon a field detachment for nothing. Those words meant that, on occasion, intelligence analysts were expected to actually go into combat zones to conduct interrogations and analyze intelligence for future actions.

Aaron reluctantly got out of bed, opened the door and Major Donnelly, a stern looking man with deep furrows on his brow and a permanent scowl on his face, barked at Aaron "Get your ass in gear boy. Go to Comstat immediately and get them to issue you a side arm and knuckle-buster. Be at HQ in 20 minutes."

The word knuckle-buster made Aaron's heart skip a beat. It was a knife, but no ordinary knife. It was a dagger for close combat and ambush situations. The clip point blade is strongly joined to the knuckle guard wrapped around brass knuckles that allowed for a firm grip to thrust the weapon deep into a man's flesh. Aaron was going into a live fire zone.

They took a truck to the airport where they boarded a helicopter and the whirring of the engine and the constant beat of the rotor blades seemed to cut into Aaron's head like a warm knife slicing butter. He could hear the blades seeming to whisper softly, "you're a dead man. You're a dead man," over and over.

Thirty minutes into the flight, the major told the five men they were going to Nha Trang. Nha

THE GIRL WHO SAID GOODBYE
FOR THE LAST TIME

Trang Aaron recalled was the place where a company of marines were wiped out by North Vietnamese forces. They were not just going up against a rag-tag army of farmers fighting for their freedom. The six men squad was going into territory filled with North Vietnamese regulars - hardened, skilled combat veterans. With the exception of the major, none of the men had ever been in combat. What was so important, thought Aaron, that they would send a military intelligence officer, a Vietnamese language specialist, an interrogator and three intelligence analysts into a live fire zone?

They landed at Nha Trang, took two rickety jeeps that looked like they were World War II surplus down winding dirt roads outside the city and waited at the base of a mountain that was surrounded by what appeared to be impenetrable jungle. After they were joined by a team of nine Green Berets who seemed to just materialize out of the jungle, the major told them that on the far side of the mountain was a North Vietnamese general's headquarters. They were there to capture him, get him to a secure area already set-up by the Green berets and interrogate him immediately, because there was word of a big North Vietnamese attack coming soon.

Though Aaron never shared the story of that night in the jungle, what follows is as accurate an account as possible, based upon the information cleaned from a variety of sources.

They traveled in jeeps on an old dirt road that went up the side of the mountain for about 45 minutes, where they stopped at the coordinates on a map the major had. They pulled the jeeps into a thicket and camouflaged them with tall grass. The major signalled for them to cross the road into the thick jungle.

Following the Green Berets into the jungle, Aaron was breathing heavily from exhaustion and anticipation. Complete silence was maintained as the party of 15 came to a sudden halt after about 30 minutes of walking through some thickets of bamboo. Aaron had cuts on his hands and the bright moonlight made the element of surprise nearly impossible. The Green Beret captain signalled for all of them to drop to the ground. Then, he motioned for two other Green Berets to move in closer to the nearby enemy encampment.

After what seemed like an eternity, one of the two men crawled back into the thicket of bamboo and flexed both his hands three times, indicating there were about 30 men in the encampment. Surely, Aaron thought to himself, they would not attack a camp with so many soldiers. However, he did not know the cunning bravado and blind devotion to duty of the Green Berets.

THE GIRL WHO SAID GOODBYE
FOR THE LAST TIME

The captain motioned for Aaron and the five others to stay right where they were. Then, the Green Berets all crawled off into the darkness as Major Donnelly motioned for the men to form a circle, so they could observe movement from any direction. They would know if it was the Green Berets coming back by three short whistles from the captain.

Aaron never knew that silence could be so deafening to the ears. The quiet was like a bomb blast at ground zero. They all knew that in a few minutes, the camp would be an inferno of calamity. Still, thought Aaron, he and his comrades were being protected from battle, because it was their job to interrogate the general and analyze the intelligence.

The first explosion lit up the darkness with bright red flames soaring skyward seeming to lick the bright moon on the horizon. Shouts and screams were heard all about. Explosions continued to rock the compound that was about 300 metres away. Aaron nervously gripped his rifle with his left hand and felt for his knife with his right. Suddenly, one of the Green Berets came tearing through the brush and one of Aaron's comrades actually fired at him but missed. The Green Beret shouted, "We are fucked, big time. There must be over 100 men in the compound. They were hiding under the main building. They came out like a swarm of locusts descending on a farmer's field. Major, get your asses out of here. There are three of us down. I have to go back in to help get them out. Your guys are too green for this. Get the hell back to the road, now."

The major, obeying an enlisted man, realized that the situation was too tenuous for men not trained as combat soldiers. He shouted, "Martin, take the point. Let's haul ass."

Aaron, his blood pumping through his heart like a raging river barrelling through a gorge, stumbled and fell, dropping his rifle. Martin was hit with a volley of fire from a thicket and did not scream as his body slammed against a large stalk of bamboo. Dead thought Aaron.

Aaron was right behind Martin, so his fall prevented him from being hit by the same volley of fire. He rolled over on his side and looked behind him. There was no one there. Apparently, the other four men had found cover. Aaron groped for his rifle but could not find it in the tall grass. All he had was his knife and side arm. The quiet was interrupted with gunfire to his right and a voice shouted, "I'm hit. I'm hit."

Aaron tried to crawl toward the position where the voice came from. He never felt so alone in his life. The grim reaper seemed to be coming for him and there was absolutely nothing he could do about it. Suddenly rocket propelled grenades whizzed overhead, landing behind Aaron. The flash of light exposed Aaron for a second and a quick burst of gunfire came his way. He rolled over on his back and remembered the infiltration course at Fort Bragg. He could do this. The jeeps were only about 100 metres away, across the road. He could crawl to them on his back.

The silence frightened Aaron more than the gunfire, because the silence meant somebody was out there, lurking in the darkness. He heard another burst of gunfire followed by a shout from a voice he recognized as the major. Three down now. It's every man for himself. A raging inferno of rocket propelled grenades whizzed overhead, exploding near the area where he heard the major.

Aaron was on his own. This was about survival, and he was determined to survive. He did not want to die in a useless war for a useless cause. He was going to get the hell out of there, go back home and tell the army to go fuck itself.

As he crawled slowly forward on his back, he had his pistol in one hand and knife in the other. Looking up at the bright moon, he made sure to stay hidden in the tall grass. He looked to his left and saw someone crawling his way. It was the enemy. Yeah thought Aaron, I have more in common with him than those brass back at the Pentagon. Knowing gunfire would give his position away; he slowly placed the revolver back in its holster and gripped the knife so tightly that he thought it would break. The guy had not seen him yet, because the moon was shining in his face. With the knife in his right hand, when the soldier was within a few feet, Aaron rolled over three or four times in his direction, startling him. As the guy tried to fire his weapon, Aaron was already lying on top of him, back to back. Aaron started jabbing his side with the knife until the guy was completely still. He could hear blood gurgling from the massive wound. Aaron had killed him silently and not given away his position. He was near the road now. Yet, the moon was so bright that any movement at all might give him away. He decided to lie there silently, waiting out the enemy until they gave up and left, thinking they had killed them all.

Aaron could not look at the man he had just killed. How ironic he thought, the two of them were lying there side-by-side like comrades, not enemies. Tears filled Aaron's eyes and he wept for the man he had just killed, but he also wept for himself, because he would have to live with that the rest of his life. As he was contemplating what he had just done, to his left, a short man came lunging toward him with a bayonet. Aaron pivoted to his right and avoided the thrust, and he shoved the knife into the man's belly as the bayonet fell harmlessly at Aaron's side. There was complete silence and Aaron waited, waited for like what seemed an eternity. As the sun came up over the horizon, all the enemy had apparently left either thinking they had killed them all or that daylight made them too vulnerable for attack from the skies.

Can you not minister to a mind diseased?
Pluck from the memory a rooted sorrow,
Raze out the written troubles of the brain,
And with some sweet oblivious antidote
Cleanse the heavy heart of that perilous stuff
which weighs upon the soul?
Sometimes the answer is no,
and it is then that the mind goes into free-fall
and drops into the abyss of despair.

That week sent Aaron's fragile state of mind into a tailspin. When he got back, he purposefully disobeyed orders and refused to target any individuals. When confronted, he would simply tell them that if they didn't like the way he was doing his job they could fire him. He still had four months left in the service, so they simply let him do menial tasks.

This led Aaron to develop an intense life-long hatred for the U.S. government, as he realized that it was no different than the other governments that were vilified for evil deeds. All the years of propaganda crystallized in his mind as a concentrated effort to brainwash the American people into supporting wars that were unnecessary. Fear was being used to control the American populace, when, in fact, the thing the American people should have feared the most was their own government.

After the army, Aaron settled down to life back in his hometown, but still had dreams of going to New York to be a private detective. It is not the purpose of this book to explore his well-known exploits in New York that have been documented in many books by his biographer, Wayne Frye. Rather, our purpose is to explore a disease of the mind that drove this defender of justice over the edge. What he had done that night to two men in order to survive caused him mental torment that would, over a period of time, be one of the many things that unravelled an already fragile mind.

A philosopher once said that the great roots of worry are conscience, fear and regret. Undoubtedly we ought to be conscious of and we ought to fear and regret evil. But if it is to be better than an impediment and harm, our worry must be largely unconscious and intuitive. The moment we become conscious of worry we are undone. Fortunately, or unfortunately, we cannot leave conscience to its own devices unless our lives are big enough and fine enough to warrant such a course. (In Aaron's case, he had a rich and full life with Jasmine Alexander, but his mental anguish kept interfering, making small things bigger than they were.) The remedy for the mental unrest, which is an illness as insidious as any, lies not in an enlightened knowledge of the harmfulness and ineffectiveness of worry over trivial matters that have little real meaning in relationships, but in the living of a life so full and good that worry cannot find a place in it. That idea of worry and conscience, that definition of serenity, simplifies life immensely. To overcome worry and mental pain by substituting development and growth need never be dull work. To know life in its farther reaches, life in its better applications, is the final remedy - the great undertaking - it is life. We must warn ourselves, not infrequently that the larger life is to be pursued for its own glorious self and not for the sake of peace. Peace may come, a peace so sure that death itself cannot shake it, but we must not expect all our affairs to run smoothly. As a matter of fact, they may run badly, but if in the end we live according to our best intuitions, we shall be justified, and we need not worry about the outcome. To put it another way, if we would have the untroubled mind, we must transfer our conscientious efforts from the small details of life, from the worry and fret of common things into another and a higher atmosphere that dignifies all relationships. We must transfigure common life, dignify it and ennoble it; then, although the old causes of worry may continue, we shall have gained a stature that will make us unconscious masters of the little troubles and in a great degree equal to the larger requirements. Life will be easier, not because we make less effort, but because we are working from another and a better level. (For Aaron, this peace of mind had come too late as he lay on his bed in the cold, dank, dingy hotel room that faithful night recalling the events which led to his downfall, with Jasmine Alexander by his side, holding his frail hand as his life ebbed away.)

THE GIRL WHO SAID GOODBYE
FOR THE LAST TIME

CHAPTER 5
HE FELT SO ASHAMED

Aaron, after divorcing his wife and moving to New York City, where he got his Private Investigator's licence, seemed to all who knew him, an extremely gregarious, self-confident man. His reputation for fighting against injustice became the stuff of legends on the seedy streets where he had his office. Even in uptown Manhattan, among the crème-de-la-crème of the city, his reputation was impeccable as a man who could be depended on in times of crisis.

Aaron seemed to be even tempered, but at times he would feel a great rage within that he kept bottled up successfully for long periods of time. He avoided most social situations, because he was uncomfortable around people and always felt inferior and unworthy of friendship. Although many people were acquainted with him, he was mostly a loner, as he experienced great solace in the privacy of his small office or apartment in lower Manhattan. In those places, he felt a certain comfort – protected and sheltered from a world that far too often overwhelmed him. When he hired B.J. Holden as his secretary, his life took a dramatic change as the statuesque beauty eventually captured his heart. Hers was a special kind of affection that saw her love the much older Aaron almost to the point of adulation.

THE GIRL WHO SAID GOODBYE
FOR THE LAST TIME

When she moved in with Aaron, she sensed he was a different man in private than in public. Though never violent with her, he would occasionally fly into a verbal assault that would reduce her to tears. She was not privy to the torment he felt from the burdens of everyday life that made him moody and unresponsive. He was building a wall around himself, a wall that shut out the normal world and happiness. From the walls of this personal prison, the sounds of discord and annoyance were thrown back at him, intensified and multiplied. The pain in his mind would sometimes become almost unbearable.

Virtues can often hide their vanquished fires within the flame of hope until conscience grows irrelevant and duty nothing but a name. Aaron wilfully fulfilled his duties as a lover and companion, but there was something missing, something that seemed to just be below the surface, and it would often boil over in recriminations and accusations hurled in anger by Aaron. This was a man on-fire inside, and there seemed to be no hope for him. He was convinced that his was a hopeless existence, as he simply waited out his time until the darkness of death would bring him peace.

Of course, for those readers who are familiar with the case of the mysterious box, B.J. Holden was eventually lost by Aaron in a way that will not

J. Wayne Frye

be explored here, because you may want to read the book, *Fall from Apocalypse*, and there is no reason to spoil the ending for you. For a while, he lived without a companion, and then he went to Stockholm on a case called by his biographer, *The Girl Who Stirred Up the Whirlwind*, and met the 26 year old Jasmine Alexander in Stockholm right after his 62nd birthday. There's was a whirlwind romance and while apart for a while, they got back together and married, settling in an upper eastside apartment.

Now, the story becomes one of deep, abiding love, but also one of a man's descent into tragic mental anguish that will make what follows more about tragedy than love – the tragedy of mental anguish that destroys a man who had everything, but whose mind deceived him into thinking happiness was unattainable. It was during the first few months of marriage that Aaron wandered about the city starved for something that he felt was missing. New York City, a megalopolis of both despair and hope, lets no man free from its grip on the soul.

From this paragraph forward, the author recalls the profound quote by Knut Hamsun *that all men hunger for that which is unattainable*. Borrowed freely from his *hunger* that made him search for a light in the darkness, what follows is an attempt to get into the mind of Aaron Adams and experience the turmoil of someone with a raging fire in the mind.

Aaron was lying awake on his sofa, having arisen at 4 AM. He often did that and just stood there watching Jasmine sleep, her chest rising methodically as a faint sigh flowed from her thick red lips that were slightly parted, seeming to invite a kiss. How he loved her. He heard the grandfather clock Jasmine had bought a few months before strike six. It was already broad daylight, and people had begun to go up and down the stairs.

From sheer force of habit, he thought it would be another day of struggle against the demons that raged within him. Despite his love for Jasmine, he could not rejoice as he was struggling against the forces of darkness. He had been somewhat hard-up lately, having no cases on his docket.

It grew lighter and lighter and Aaron took to reading the advertisements in the old newspaper on the coffee table. He heard the clock strike seven as he got up and put on his clothes, being extra quiet, so as to not awaken Jasmine from her slumber.

He exited the bedroom, strolled toward the window, raised it about half-way up and looked out. From where he was standing, he saw a vibrant city coming alive, beginning to teem with activity.

THE GIRL WHO SAID GOODBYE
FOR THE LAST TIME

He leaned out and gazed upon people of all shapes, sizes and colours beginning their days, and most seemed happy to be strolling in the bright morning sun. The ever increasing noise in the streets seemed to be whispering, "These people are happy, these people are truly alive, embracing life with vigour." However, for Aaron the city and the apartment was a coffin with the lid closed on his despair.

He had a handful of puffed wheat for breakfast, as he sat forlornly at the kitchen bar, swivelling from side to side on the stool. He thought back over his years and all the promise that he showed as a youth, but now he was old, tired and weary of the battle of life. Yet, he had to muster the courage to face another day, because his life was in the bedroom, sleeping soundly, expecting her champion to always be there for her. She had said to the much older Aaron before their marriage that it was almost as if she was born the day he came into her life. He was as much a father to her as a husband. She depended on him for guidance through the perils of life.

For years Aaron had fought an uphill battle with despair. He often sat at his desk, writing stories about a fictional detective. They were strange ideas and farcical sojourns for his restless mind. As soon as one piece was finished, he immediately started on another. Getting rejected by publishers was a regular occurrence, but occasionally, he would find some small firm that was interested in publishing his books for no advance and a minimum royalty. So, even his ability to write well-constructed literature made him feel like a failure, because he was not a famous author.

He walked over to the kitchen sink and let the cold water pour into his cupped hands and took a sip. He strolled back to the bedroom and looked again at Jasmine as she slept peacefully. Her naked body was a thing of delight, but long ago, Aaron's passionate ardour had faded into the oblivion of lost hope. He left the apartment and almost glided, rather than walked down the spiral staircase. The roll of vehicles and hum of voices filled the air, a mighty morning-choir mingled with the rapid footsteps of people headed to their little cubicles of enslavement to the corporations that ruled supreme in a land of broken dreams and promises. The clamouring and vibrancy of the city gave him no feeling of exhilaration. He fell to observing and trying to analyze the people who passed by him as he walked slower than normal. What were they thinking? Were they like Aaron, lonely and out of place in a city of millions?

He went on through the streets listlessly, without troubling himself about anything at all, stopped aimlessly at a corner, turned off into a side street without having any reason for going there. It was just something to do. He actually dreaded going to his office for another day of lost hope that the next big case would materialize, and that would once again make headlines in the paper, and he would be proclaimed a champion of justice. It happened often, but it meant little to Aaron, as he cloistered himself in his cocoon of lost hope and fought against despair.

He could hear people panting from exertion as they passed him. A man passed with a large brown bag under his arms. Why was he in such a hurry? What was so important? An old crippled man was wobbling labouredly in front of him. Aaron looked forlornly at him and thought how lucky he was at his age not to be infirm. Yet, it seemed not to ease the pain he felt, the pain he struggled with each day in his mind.

He purposely slowed down so he could follow the man. Why? Perhaps it was because the old man gave Aaron a bit of exuberance over the fact that, as the old saying goes, "there but by the grace of God go I."

Aaron turned down lower 5th Avenue where it was not a street filled with the affluent barons of greed, but rather, a teeming slum of desperate people who were the victims of an economic system that let all the wealth flow to those at the top. Disgusted with the poverty and hopelessness before him, he decided to go over to Boutin Avenue and sit in the park.

He found a bench to himself, and just sat, staring into the nothingness. All about him were the poor souls who had been discarded by an uncaring society where bombs and bullets were more important than feeding the hungry. Oh, the hunger, the hunger Aaron felt for peace within.

Aaron got up again and began his aimless stroll. He overtook two ladies, and as he did so, he brushed one of them accidentally on the arm. He said, pardon me." And with her full ruby red lips she softly replied, "No problem."

Aaron felt, as he passed the lady, that for some reason she was staring at him. Was it because she thought him a dirty old man? Was it because she found his looks disgusting? He tried to pull himself together and proceeded on his way; his legs began to jerk under him, his gait became unsteady as self-doubts raged in his mind? Yes, he was old and ugly. People found him disgusting, unworthy of their time.

Walking up to his second floor office in a building off 5th Avenue, on the stairs he met a woman with a huge pocketbook in her right hand. She squeezed diffidently against the wall to make room for Aaron as if he had a contagious disease and she must avoid touching him. There was a scowl on her face as she proceeded past him. Why? Why did she find him so distasteful a person?

It was about twelve o'clock. Aaron could not do it. He simply could not go into his dank, barren little office. He turned and headed back down the stairs.

He headed to uptown Manhattan, where the smart set was taking their lunch breaks. He noticed how gaily and lightly people he passed carried their radiant heads and swung themselves through life as through it was a ball-room. There was no sorrow in a single look he met, no burden on any shoulder, perhaps not even a clouded thought, not a little hidden pain in any of the happy souls. Aaron hugged those thoughts as he continued his journey to nowhere. Insignificant incidents, miserable details of perceived slights and lack of love from people forced their way into his imagination and scattered about in a hopeless torrent of despair that wracked his brain.

It was as if some phantom were following him, whisking about overhead as a ghostly apparition. Why had the hand of fate turned against him? Why against him? Was not he a kind, generous and loving person? Why did he suffer the fit of rage within his soul?

THE GIRL WHO SAID GOODBYE
FOR THE LAST TIME

He asked himself if he was paying for all the individuals he had targeted for assassination when he was an intelligence analyst in the army? Or was it for the two people he had killed that night in the thicket to escape certain death? From the time he was a little boy, he felt ill-luck was his destiny. He could clearly notice he was gradually increasing in debilities; he had become too languid to control or lead himself from the dark pit into which he was falling. He felt like someone had bored a way into his soul and hollowed him out. There was only emptiness.

Was he intended for annihilation like the people he had targeted for annihilation in Vietnam? His whole being was at that moment in the highest degree of torture. He felt the weight of an anvil pressing down upon his shoulders. The people who came and went around him glided past like faint gleams of light. He strolled toward Central Park where found a seat by the duck pond.

Aaron wished he believed in God, because only a God could assuage his despair. He felt as if his brains were spilling out of his head, leaving a deep, dark, empty vacuum. Damn he thought. Damn this despair that envelopes me and embraces my soul.

He grew bitterer about his afflictions of despair. Why were obstacles to happiness always put between him and that which he should have? He looked up towards the sky and cursed his fate. He felt like shaking his fist at the God in which he did not believe.

Everything around him was suddenly a distraction. Gnats were flittering all about, and he brushed them away with a flick of the hand. He let his eyes glide down to his chest and noticed he was breathing heavily. His gaze continued downward and he noticed the jerking movement his foot made each time his heart beat. Suddenly a feeling of recognition trembled through his senses; the tears welled up in his eyes, and a soft voice seemed to whisper "you are weak. You are weak!" He closed his eyes and the physical tears dried up, but inside he was bawling in sorrow.

He felt a sudden gust of wind as his mind raced over the mood swings that had plagued him for three years. Seventeen years with Jasmine had been euphoric and filled with mirth and laughter, with a few intermittent mood swings, but the last three years had been like a torrent of despair for her as she watched Aaron seemingly disintegrate before her eyes. How long would she tolerate it? Aaron, himself, had taught her to stand up for herself and to never suffer any indignity. Yet, she suffered indignities from him because of her deep love for him. But how much longer could she take it?

THE GIRL WHO SAID GOODBYE
FOR THE LAST TIME

A small man sat on the bench with him, and unfolded a newspaper. The insane idea entered Aaron's head that it might be a quite particular newspaper, even unique. His curiosity increased, and he began to move backwards and forwards on the seat. It might be dangerous documents about a conspiracy as sinister as 9/11. Come on, he thought, you are being ridiculous.

The man sat quietly and pondered over his newspaper. On the far side, near the armrest of the bench, was a small brown package with a white string tied around it. Aaron began to wonder what was in it.

Suddenly, the man turned to Aaron and said, "Nice day isn't it?"

Aaron, thinking to himself, it was just another one of those abysmal days, masked his discontent and replied, "Yes it is."

Feeling disconcerted by the man's presence, Aaron arose. As he started to leave, the old man said, "I think I have seen you in the park with that lovely lady on your arm?"

Aaron, realizing that all men found something alluring and exciting about Jasmine, could not help but swell with pride when he answered, "yes."

THE GIRL WHO SAID GOODBYE
FOR THE LAST TIME

There was more to Jasmine than physical beauty, her inner beauty shined with a peaceful tranquility that radiated like a blazing sun on a hot July day. She was the morning dew on the ripening grape. She was the crescendo of a rousing symphony. She was the mischievous smile on a precocious child's lips. She was Aaron's life.

"Is that your wife," the old man asked.

Aaron, swelling with pride, said, "She is, for 20 years."

"So lovely," replied the old man.

Lovely, thought Aaron. She was beauteous; she was sinfully fascinating. Eyes like raw silk, arms of amber. Just one glance from her was as seductive as a kiss; and when she called his name, her voice seemed to be floating on a cloud. And why shouldn't she be so beautiful? She was simply an angel of light floating gracefully down from heaven.

The man had rose wobbly, snatched his parcel from off the seat, said "goodbye" and left with the tottering steps of an old man.

Aaron sat back down, leaned back and looked at the retreating figure that seemed to shrink at each step as it passed away. Aaron did not know from

J. Wayne Frye   73

THE GIRL WHO SAID GOODBYE
FOR THE LAST TIME

where the impression came, but it appeared to him that the stoop shouldered old man would be him in a year or two. That would be his fate. He was already 80 and had suffered two strokes and was a diabetic. Yet, he continued in his lonely profession.

The day began to decline, the sun sank and a slight breeze began to rustle the leaves on the trees. Aaron closed his eyes, and got more and more sleepy. He gradually dozed off, but sprang immediately up, realizing it was getting late. He had wasted a day.

Aaron felt himself to be like a creeping thing on the verge of destruction, gripped by ruin in the midst of a whole world ready for lethargic sleep. He rose, oppressed by weird terrors, and took some furious strides down the path out of the park as he said to himself, "Enough of this melancholia."

Exiting the park, Aaron noticed the wind was picking up. He must get home to Jasmine, who may have called the office several times and was now worried about him. She was like that. For 20 years, she had doted on him.

He wrapped himself in her warm arms and felt a reassurance that his melancholia would subside with her near him. Although now old, Aaron was still active and continued to go to work every day, even though there were now very few clients.

He woke very early in the next morning. It was still quite dark as he opened his eyes. He looked over at Jasmine's naked body and wished for his virility just one more time, so that he might plant his seed in her moist mound of desire. Aaron, gently touching Jasmine's hip, rose and walked into the living room and over to his desk where he sat down and began to write. It was as if a vein had burst in him; one word follows another, and they fit themselves together harmoniously with telling effect. Scene piles on scene, actions and speeches bubble up in his brain, and a wonderful sense of pleasure empowers him. He wrote as one possessed, and filled page after page, with prose that flowed like vintage wine into crystal.

It grew lighter, and Jasmine came into the room, placed her hands on his shoulders and said, "Good morning, dear."

For no reason, Aaron blurted out, "Good, what is so good about it? It is just another day of misery that will not end soon enough for me."

Having lived with Aaron's increasing mood swings, Jasmine said nothing. She only left in silence, once again wondering what inner demons made him act so irrationally at times. She was witnessing the disintegration of the one she loved dearly, and her heart ached for the man she once knew.

An intense, peculiar melancholia often emanated from fantasies of Aaron's mind. He realized his harsh behaviour was inappropriate, went to Jasmine and said, "I apologize. I do not know what drives such an occasional rage in me. I know my episodes are getting worse. I am an old man, so you will not have to put up with it much longer."

As always, Jasmine said, "It is alright Aaron, don't worry about it."

However, deep inside she knew that she was nearing the end of a rope that was strangling her. She loved him dearly, but the episodes were affecting her mental state, as well.

The morning was gloomy and wet; which was no help to Aaron's deteriorating state of mind. The streets were glistening from the rain which had fallen in the early morning. The sky hung damp and heavy over the city, and there was no glint of sunlight visible. It would be another day of gloom.

Aaron began to wander about among the people in the street, again wondering why so many of them seemed happy. The rain stopped, so he

THE GIRL WHO SAID GOODBYE
FOR THE LAST TIME

wandered to the park, wiped the wetness off the bench and took a seat. He sighed and thought he should actually go to his office today. He had not been on a case in almost three months. No matter how famous he once was, people just didn't want to hire an 80 year old gumshoe. He was only fooling himself. It was over for him. All he had left was his writing, and even that seemed to be fading away, as he struggled more and more for words and the publisher kept having him edit and re-edit. .

Aaron thought was there possibly a hole somewhere to be found where he could creep in and hide himself from life? Visions; senseless dreams! Aaron had not eaten in three days as he could not stomach food, because something was tearing at his insides, seemingly causing a raging fire not only in his head, but in the rest of his body.

The day seemed to race away as the great spirit of darkness spread a shroud over Aaron. Everything was silent - everything. But there was a symphony of symbols playing in Aaron's head, no, not a symphony, a funeral dirge. He got up and shuffled off toward home in the gloom and agony of despair. When would it end?

Fury welled up in Aaron, blazing with brutal strength. He was becoming mentally and physically more and more unstable. Each day, he sank deeper into the morass of despair.

In the dark abyss of the mind, angry demons bristle with range to make the pain unbearable. Aaron placed his hands over his ears, got up and began walking. He quickened his pace, almost fearing that some unknown beast was stalking him.

He was now desperately dragging one foot after the other. He felt an intense scorching heat in his head, and his temples pulsated. He rounded a corner, stepped into the alley and threw up, heaving vast quantities of green matter that fell at his feet.

He felt a gnawing in his chest, so he sat down on a bus bench exhausted, as he put his elbows on his knees and his head in his hands. He sat for a long time as the wind blew lustily through the elm trees around him, and the day began to decline into darkness.

He walked up the street not going in any particular direction. The wind freshened, the clouds chased madly across the sky dancing in joyful merriment, and they gradually disappeared as it got darker. He walked, and began to cry for no reason. An hour passed; passed with such strange slowness, such weariness. He stood in front of a department store window for about ten minutes, thinking that Jasmine would be worried.

Getting home, he noticed the place was dark. On the dining room table was an envelope with the word *Aaron* written on it. He slowly picked it up and placed it in the breast pocket of his coat. Slowly, quite slowly he left the apartment head hung low, because he knew what was in the letter and he did not want to read it. The letter was the end. Yes, the end of his life with Jasmine. She was leaving him. He knew what the letter said.

All through the night, until the cloudy dawn, Aaron walked the streets in despair. He felt his life ebbing away. There was emptiness deep within him, and he was untouched by all around him. He had descended into his own little world. He sat down and put his feet up on the seat and leaned over. He felt isolated and alone. Only the lonely, crooning voice of silence struck in monotones on his ears, and the dark monsters in his mind drew him into a cocoon of darkness. His thoughts raced like a hurricane coming ashore in the gulf.

"If only the hurt would go away," cried Aaron to himself. There never was any end to his misery as he cursed the darkness of his mind. He would not go back home. He could no longer live in the place that he had shared with his beloved Jasmine. He got up and stumbled down the street.

THE GIRL WHO SAID GOODBYE
FOR THE LAST TIME

His hunger was now tormenting him as much as the demons of the mind. He reached into his pants and pulled out his wallet. He never carried much money, usually no more than $20. Of course, he had plenty of credit cards. As he started to look inside to see how much money he had, a brazen thief whizzed by like a flash of lightning, grabbing his wallet and heading up the path. Now, Aaron had no wallet, no money and he was alone on the streets with nowhere to go, because he could not face the emptiness he would feel if he went back home and Jasmine was not there. He reached into his pants pockets and pulled out a measly 35 cents.

Aaron was like so many others in the vast wasteland of capitalism, where only the wealthy survive unscathed by life's hardships. Aaron was to taste poverty for the first time in his life. He railed at himself for not being stronger. He was now a defeated old man.

It began to rain, and he felt the water soak through his clothes, chilling him so badly that he began to shiver. He needed a hotel and a warm bed, but he had no money or credit cards and he could not bring himself to go back home.

In the land of "you're on your own," there is little respite for the poor and weary that trod the streets not of gold, but of broken dreams and heartache. Aaron stood in a doorway, and a policeman swinging a night stick said, "Move on old man, no loitering in doorways."

There was no sympathy from those commissioned by the privileged class to enforce the law. Only the privileged avoided persecution and shame. How did America tackle poverty? It simply made it a crime.

Aaron shuffled down the street, seemingly aged many years in only a few hours. He was now part of the vast throngs who had to search for shelter and food in a nation of plenty. The problem was it was only plentiful for those at the top of the economic ladder.

Aaron stopped in front of another department store, trying to clear his head of the enormity of the problem he faced. Another policeman strolled by as the rain mixed with snow began to fall in torrents. Turning to Aaron, the stocky man said, "You have a place to stay?"

Aaron replied, "No sir."

"Well then, let's find you a place old fellow. I'll take you to a shelter in the bowery.

The policeman dropped Aaron off at the Holy Redeemer Shelter. The supervisor asked Aaron his name, but Aaron, realizing someone might recognize his name, decided to lie. "Tony Tognetti," he replied.

"You have an occupation?"

Aaron, now realizing how cold and heartless the man seemed, replied, "Do you think if I had an occupation I would be here?"

The man did not reply to Aaron's snide remark. He just pointed toward a door and said, "Through there, find an empty cot and go to sleep. If you have any valuables, check them with me and you can pick them up in the morning."

Aaron, now fed up with the arrogance of those who served the poor but looked with disdain on them, replied, "Yeah, I have the Hope Diamond, but I like to look at it before I go to bed," as he shuffled off to the dormitory and took a cot in the back, pulling up the blanket and warming his chilled body. He was home now. This was all he would know from now on.

Aaron lay in the darkness, hoping that sleep would come to him, but it did not. He thought back on all the cruel things he had said to Jasmine, and wished he could go back and correct his mistakes, but it was too late. She had grown tired and weary of his mood swings and finally reached her breaking point.

THE GIRL WHO SAID GOODBYE
FOR THE LAST TIME

Aaron gazed into the darkness and a dense mass of gloom descended upon him. There was no bottom to the pit into which he had fallen. It was bottomless this time.

Was this to be the destiny of New York's most famous detective? Was he destined to live out what he had left of life in filth and squalor? Of course he would. This was America.

A pall of doom descended upon Aaron as he gazed up at the ceiling and thought it was no ordinary ceiling. It was slowly moving down toward him, ready to crush him. It was the lid on his coffin, closing over him.

He simply could not fall asleep. The rain and snow had ceased outside, and he could not hear a sound except for faint footsteps in the street.

Aaron was thirsty, so he got up to look for a water fountain. He groped precariously in the darkness, seeing one man going through the pockets of one of his fellow sojourners down the path of despair. Aaron ignored him and continued to grope in the darkness.

His mind was confused. Finally giving up on finding a water fountain, he went back to bed and forced himself to close his eyes. He lay there without making a movement, sweated and felt his blood jerk violently through his veins. His heart was pounding furiously as he moaned and started to cry.

The darkness claimed him; the unfathomable black eternity surrounded him. He had never seen a night so black. How dark it was! He thought of dark monsters waiting to devour him and chew on his soul. He wanted to cry out in terror, as he clutched the bed tightly, frightened like a little child confounded with nightmarish dreams. He glimpsed upwards again. He felt it must be daylight, felt it through every pore in his body as the sun's rays twinkled on the skylight. He felt relief that the darkness was fading.

Then night drug on until a more jovial man than the night clerk went through the dormitory pounding on an old pot, shouting, "Everybody up. Prayer session and then breakfast."

Aaron thought to himself that everyone had to take a dose of Jesus with their bread. Where was Jesus when Aaron was descending into the black pit of hell?

After prayer and breakfast, Aaron was ushered into the street. Jesus only had so much compassion. You had to spend the day scurrying about in the streets. The day was bright and the sun's rays felt good to Aaron.

THE GIRL WHO SAID GOODBYE
FOR THE LAST TIME

Without knowing it, Aaron was on his way home. Arriving at his apartment building he looked up and cried. There was a police car parked out front. The McCaully's must have had another fight thought Aaron.

He stood and turned something over in his mind before he ventured doing it. Should he find his beloved and ask for mercy from her? No, he could not do that. She had suffered enough. He turned and strolled back toward the bowery, an old man defeated by the demons of the mind.

That day, Aaron, still using the name Tony Tognetti, was given a voucher for a hotel room in a dilapidated building in the lower bowery. The city would pick up the tab, but he had to share the room with another man. They could eat at the Holy Redeemer Shelter.

Exhausted, Aaron flung himself on the old metal bed with a mattress that sunk in the middle and actually laughed at his situation. Who would have ever dreamed that this could happen to Aaron Adams?

The acrid smell of cigarette smoke filtered under the door into the room. Loud shouting could be heard down the hallway, and someone kept shouting, "fuck you" out in the hall. Yeah, thought Aaron, who had the energy for sex in this place?

THE GIRL WHO SAID GOODBYE
FOR THE LAST TIME

Aaron opened the window to let in some fresh air. His roommate was brought up to the room, a man of maybe 60 who asked where the bathroom was. His escort said, "Each end of the hall. Showers are available, but you have to furnish your own soap."

The man replied sarcastically, "Don't need to shower. I'll just get dirty again," as he looked over at Aaron who was observing the two men and said, "what the hell is your problem, buddy."

Aaron, feeling a bit of that old bravado which he was famous for, replied, "Keep running your mouth off buddy and you'll find out. I may be old, but I still know where to kick a man to get him to shut up."

The guy grinned and said, "tough old geezer, uh?"

Aaron, now feeling like a man again, said, "You don't want to find out how tough, buddy."

The escort said, "You two better learn how to get along. You'll be roommates for a while."

Aaron said nothing as the escort left. The sun gleamed in through the window, and he could hear the sounds of people filtering up from the street below. This was his home now. He wanted no one to find him, no one to see the depths of despair to which he had sunk.

Aaron reached in his breast coat pocket and pulled out the envelope that Jasmine had left. He fondled it, as if it offered him an opportunity to be near her, to smell her fresh scent after she got out of the shower, to rest his face in her black hair and pull her to him, feeling her warmth. The envelope had gotten wet, so he placed it on the night table beside his bed to dry. He could not bring himself to open it. It would be too painful.

Aaron got up and started wandering up and down the room. How depressing everything looked. Small scraps of the carpet had been torn out and the bare floor showed through. There were wooden two chairs, but not even one picture on the bare walls. A few sheets of paper had been crumbled up and tossed in the far corner.

The other man rolled over, got up, walked over to the table and started to pick up Aaron's envelope. Aaron, in his no nonsense tone, said, "I wouldn't advise messing with that buddy. It would be too big a price to pay."

The guy pulled back his hand, walked back to his bed and lay down. Aaron walked over, picked up the envelope and fondled it gently before putting it back in his inside breast pocket.

THE GIRL WHO SAID GOODBYE
FOR THE LAST TIME

Aaron left and started trudging through the bowery, passing by the discards of society who sat in boarded up doorways with beer cans between their knees, eating the junk called food by corporations, or puffing cigarettes that kept the corporate CEO's of the tobacco companies in their uptown 10 million dollar condos, all bought for them on the backs of addicted people who fell for the corporate marketing that enslaved them. Aaron saw an open doorway, so he decided to wander in. He climbed the dilapidated stairwell to the second floor and observed where the poor and downtrodden were expected to survive.

He was fatigued, so he sat down on the floor, exhausted from his physical plight but more exhausted from his mental state. There was a tear in his right eye as he thought about going home, but knew he could not. An hour passed as he stoically sat in the one spot, his knees pulled up, his elbows on his kneecaps and his head bowed as if in prayer. A numb feeling of drowsiness brought a brief slumber.

He snapped to life when someone barked, "Out of here you bum."

Aaron, too tired for a retort, got up and went outside. He clenched his hands together and wished he were home, but he had no home anymore.

THE GIRL WHO SAID GOODBYE
FOR THE LAST TIME

He took a few strides down the street, and stopped again. Before he realized it, he was at the railway station in the lower bowery near the docks. A faint sweat forced itself out on his face, and trickled down his eyelids. He turned and walked over to the wharf. He stood there and contemplated his fate, wondering how much longer he would have to endure breathing.

The ships of commerce were being unloaded by some of the few union workers left in a country that thought unions were nothing but an opening for that dreaded socialism that gave everybody a fair shot. There was bustle and movement everywhere, constant shouting and a smell of economic servitude about the place. An old woman sat near Aaron on the wharf, giving him a toothless grin. Aaron nodded back, but could not muster a smile.

Vendors selling everything from Twinkies to cough medicine scurried up and down the docks hoping to pick up some change for a fix, a cig or a bottle of wine.

Aaron sat there contemplating where an old man his age would eventually wind up. He would die alone in some hovel or at a charity hospital where the poor and forgotten were carted off to be tossed away like the useless human beings society thought they were.

THE GIRL WHO SAID GOODBYE
FOR THE LAST TIME

Aaron was coming to the realization that he had sunk to the depths of despair that never were imaginable. Yet, he no longer really cared. All he had lived for was gone. There was nothing left for him.

It was now 3 o'clock and Aaron had eaten nothing all day, but his insides were on fire. How could he eat? Aaron moved down the wharf and struggled up a staircase leading to the street. He stood at the top of the stairs and asked himself, "What am I to do now? Is this the way I will spend my last days?

A fountain pen lay at his feet. He stooped down and picked it up. What use did he have for a pen? He had nothing to write or anybody to write to. He was a worn out man.

Someone ascended the stairs. It was a man nearly as old as Aaron. He was panting, out of breath. Aaron reached over and took him by the arm to lead him to a nearby bench. The man thanked him. Aaron, without responding, wandered off down the street in search of the peace he had never found.

Aaron's pace was brisk and sure until he arrived at his hotel. There, he stood still, almost ready to cry with vexation at not being able to muster the energy to go in and ascend the stairs. He trembled and had to force himself to keep standing. He managed to get himself into the foyer, where an old worn out sofa offered respite from his exhaustion.

He dried the sweat off my face, and drew great refreshing breaths, sucking in the air he needed to revive himself. He sat for at least 30 minutes. People came and went, never even showing concern for an old man breathing heavily. Why should they?

How bleak things looked for Aaron. He was tired and worn out as he had never been before in his life. He sat there contemplating how he had arrived at this point in his life. How low he had sunk, because of the fire that raged within him, a fire he could not control. He looked down at his wrists and saw that his veins were protruding more than usual. His heart was pumping furiously. Now thought Aaron, I am going to die. He whispered to himself, "what difference does it make, I am already dead."

He finally managed to make it upstairs where he washed himself by standing under the shower and letting the water cascade over his aching body. He walked to his room naked, carrying his clothes, because he no longer cared about his dignity. He lay himself down gently on the bed. Suddenly, he felt a burst of energy, blood rushed to his head and he got a violent palpitation of the heart. He was not scared, but wondered if this was it? Was this truly the end?

Time passed slowly and Aaron could no longer sleep, so he got up and went out to wander the city again. He let himself sink upon one of the seats by a Catholic church with demons and gargoyles on it. He was apathetic, weary, sick and exhausted by events over which he felt he had no control. He was not living; he was passing time.

Hour after hour went by and the lights of the city began to fade as a dense fog rolled in from the bay and snow flurries flittered about. Aaron's chest felt like it had a hole in it. He suffered fearfully from the angst of his hopelessness.

He sat as still as a statue, not stirring, seemingly not even breathing. He hardly moved, and didn't even blink an eye. People came and went; the noise of cars, the tramp of feet, and chatter of tongues filled the air.

At last he got up, dragging himself slowly to his feet, and reeled down the streets wobbling like a drunken man.

A pair of lovers stood in a doorway and talked together softly; a little farther up a girl popped her head out of a window. He walked so slowly and thoughtfully, that he seemed to be floating like a spectre.

A prostitute came out of a doorway and said, "Want me to play with it old man? How about five bucks?"

Aaron, who long ago had given up sex, shook his head no and the woman eased back into the doorway.

His face seemed hot and he wondered if he had a fever. His cheeks were dark and sunken; his eyes had a blank stare of nothingness, as if they were glass. He reached up and felt his face. He did not realize how much weight he had lost. His cheeks were like two soup bowls, they were sunken and hollow. He stopped at a store window and looked at a man who was unrecognizable. Was this really Aaron Adams?

His eyes were sinking right into his head. His brow was deeply wrinkled and the flesh seemed to be just hanging there, waiting to drop off. He was a walking deformity of the mind.

He felt a spasm in his right leg and it twitched for what seemed like several minutes. He leaned against the window and felt its dampness and it felt good on his hot face. With steadily increasing frequency, people strolled by, but looked away from the grim creature that stood before a window sighing. He rolled his forehead on the window and the coldness exhilarated him for a few seconds.

Someone actually looked at him and said, "Disgusting!"

Another man whispered to his female companion, "now that old man is what I call a real derelict."

For some reason Aaron thought of Dr. Davis, who years ago had tried to help him cope with his depression. Yet, not even he understood the depths of Aaron's pain.

Was Aaron mad? Yes, he thought, I am mad. He felt the coarseness of the madness in his blood, felt it darting pain through his brain. So this was to be the end of him! He slowly resumed his painful walk. He needed to find a haven of rest.

Aaron felt a growing fear. He saw himself imprisoned in a dark cell with padding on the walls, pacing back and forth, pacing back and forth. Not that! No, not that, please.

He promised to the darkness around him that he would pull himself out of it, make himself whole again. Some remedy for his predicament would turn up!

THE GIRL WHO SAID GOODBYE
FOR THE LAST TIME

He stumbled on, as he wept with emotion. Suddenly he thought of his friend Bruce, the one man who had an understanding of his pain, because he had been in so much despair himself but had risen from the depth of darkness to find light. Yes, he would find Bruce.

He lived far away, but he could make it. He knew he could. Aaron struggled toward Bruce's apartment building. When he got there he just stood and stared at it. He told himself that he had become loathsome, and he did not want Bruce to see him in this condition. He turned and headed back up town, keeping his eyes on lamppost after lamppost, steadily moving onward, but to where? Was he walking to his doom?

Suddenly Aaron's knees trembled fearfully, and he stopped to support himself against a lamppost. Filling with determination, he started once again putting one foot in front of another but going where?

He was sick with hunger all of a sudden, but he had no money. Perhaps he could find a shelter where they were serving dinner. He thought of himself as no more than a dog in search of a bone. There must be an end of this! It had really gone all wrong for him. He had held himself up for many years, stood erect through so many hard times, and now, all at once, Aaron Adams was going to beg for sustenance. This one day had coarsened his whole mind, bespattered his soul with shamelessness.

He saw the Holy Redeemer soup kitchen in the distance. That gave him renewed strength. It was almost 7:00 o'clock he noticed as he looked at the clock on the Dime Savings Bank Building. He had to hurry, they stopped serving at 7.

He stumbled and fell. He lay there for a few minutes and looked at the clock again, 7:05. He had not made it. Well, he had done all he could. To think that he really could not succeed once in a whole day! If he told it no one could believe it; if he were to write it down they would say he had invented it. Not a single place was open to him all day! It was a wasted day by an old man who felt like garbage in the gutter. Hope was fading fast. If all hope was over, there was an end of it at least, an end called death.

He took his time and crept home at a slow snail's pace. He felt thirsty, luckily for the first time through the whole day, and he went and sought about for a place where he could get a drink. He was a long distance away from the park and the water fountain. It would take a quarter of an hour to walk to the park. He was not at all so certain that he could wait, so parched was his throat. There he stood, stock-still, and he commenced to smile. Maybe there was a remedy to his predicament. He looked over at a large pool of water near the curb in a hole that had been made in the sidewalk. He bent down and drank from it. Yes, he was really a dog now, he thought.

He reached into his pocket and felt a coin. Yes, a coin. He might eat something after all. He pulled it out, only a measly quarter. He saw a coffee shop. Maybe he could get just a piece of bread for a quarter.

He walked into the diner, and noticed there were only three people sitting at the counter. All three looked at him with disgust. As the waitress came over, she chortled, "What ya want, buddy?"

"I, I am hungry. I have a quarter. Could I just have a piece of bread?"

"You kidding me? Toast is $2.00. That's the cheapest bread we got. A quarter ain't gonna get ya nothing."

The three patrons shook their heads and Aaron turned, his shoulders stooped, took a deep breath and walked out the door. The cooling night air seemed to smack his face with a chill. The only thing left was back to that dank and dirty room, where he would lay and hope for merciful death. Yes, it would be better than going on like this.

THE GIRL WHO SAID GOODBYE
FOR THE LAST TIME

He saw a man sitting on a bench eating a snickers bar. Should he? Should he go over and ask to buy a bite for a quarter? He was shivering with fear, and his heart beat like a sledge-hammer. He looked down at the snickers bar. He could almost taste the chocolate.

The man looked up and smiled as he took a bite out of the candy bar. He shook his head, and took the small piece of candy that was left and threw it on the sidewalk a few feet away. He then laughed as Aaron bent over and picked it up. Only a small morsel thought Aaron, so he tried to make two bites out of the little piece of candy. So good, so good. Yes, it was sustenance at last, even though only a little.

Suddenly Aaron saw a pawn shop, and he remembered he had a pair of reading glasses in his inside coat pocket. He reached in and gently felt the envelope that Jasmine had left, as he pulled out his glasses.

He walked into the junk-laden pawn shop, and the clerk looked at his face without saying anything. Aaron was scared, but sure he had brought something of which the man would have an interest.

"Well," said the clerk as he looked with disdain at Aaron.

THE GIRL WHO SAID GOODBYE
FOR THE LAST TIME

Aaron thrust the glasses toward the clerk. The clerk shook his head and pointed toward a glass case filled with reading glasses. Aaron said, "how about 50 cents?"

Upon this, the pawnbroker burst out laughing, and returned to his desk without saying a word. There stood Aaron; he had not hoped for much, yet, all the same, he had thought of the possibility of being helped. That laughter seemed to be a death-warrant, as the pawn-broker said, "You know quite well I can't lend you anything on those glasses. Take a hike old man."

Mechanically, Aaron put the glasses back in his pocket again, feeling the envelope he had never opened. It seemed to have the warmth of his beloved Jasmine. Turning away, Aaron lowered his head and walked out.

While he stood outside the pawnshop, lost in thought, a man passed by and was preparing to enter the shop. He had given Aaron a little shove as he gripped the door and said, "Pardon me." Then, he squinted his eyes and stared at Aaron.

"Is that you?" he said, suddenly. "Damn, man, is that you Aaron?"

Losing all his pride, Aaron admitted who he was. "Yes, it is I. I had business in the pawnshop."

THE GIRL WHO SAID GOODBYE
FOR THE LAST TIME

Aaron recognized the man as a derelict whom he had helped once while on a case in the bowery. Yes, it was Kurt Kelby, but he could be of no help. He was almost as destitute as Aaron, and was a chronic alcoholic. With a shaking voice Aaron said, "Oh, I had business as I said. Just went in to ask a few questions as I am on a case. You are going in too, I see."

"Yes, but I can't believe you would be dressed in rags standing in front of a pawn shop. What were you trying to pawn?"

Aaron's knees trembled; he supported himself against the wall and said, "I wanted to pawn some reading glasses. It is all I have left of value, but it is of no use to the pawnbroker."

"What the hell!" he cried. "I can't believe this."

"Good-night!" said Aaron as he turned and started to walk away. He could feel the tears starting to well up now and he was fighting to keep his dignity.

"Wait a minute," Kilby said.

What was Aaron expected to wait for? Was he not on the road to oblivion?

"Yes," replied Aaron, "if you will be out soon."

J. Wayne Frye

THE GIRL WHO SAID GOODBYE
FOR THE LAST TIME

"Of course" he broke in, seizing hold of Aaron's arm; "but I may as well tell you that I don't believe you. It is better you come in along with me."

Kilby pawned a watch and took Aaron for a meal at a hole-in-the-wall restaurant. The evening was actually pleasant, but Aaron slipped away when Kilby went to the washroom. He felt so ashamed.

CHAPTER 6
NOBODY KNOWS, NOBODY CARES

The agony of Aaron continued unabated as he felt a sickening emptiness inside, but he could not go in supplication to his beloved Jasmine and beg her to wrap her arms around him and take him back into her warm bosom of hope. He did not want her to see him as a weak old man with no hope. She deserved better.

For almost a week, he stayed in his hotel, turning from side to side on the dingy bed, and occasionally staring at the ceiling when he would pause and lie on his back. The air was dank and smelled of decay. Was Aaron decaying? Was he beginning to decompose as he breathed?

The room began to whirl about in his mind and he recalled the interludes of lovemaking with Jasmine that had been an incredible adjunct to a deep, abiding love between the two. Before Jasmine he had only existed, not lived. Ah, sweet love. The memory of the years flowed by as he lay there contemplating what he had lost. His recollection of romantic interludes began to overwhelm him as felt a bulge in his pants.

He recalled the first time they had sex, and tears welled up in his eyes as his mind returned to those golden times 20 years before. "My dear Aaron," said Jasmine as she looked at his stiffness. "I will do my best to relieve you of that painful bulge. Get up, shut the door, and come to my bed to enjoy my warmth that awaits you with great anticipation. I am exploding with desire. Come and get it my lovely Aaron."

He instantly complied, and she commenced to slide her nightgown off as she lay on the bed. Every detail of her charming body devoured his greedy eyes. Her smooth, glossy, and abundant hair that cascaded down over her shoulders touched the tips of her nipples. She looked divine. She reached out with both her arms as she spread her legs wide and enticed him to get on top of her.

She whispered, "Place yourself on your knees between my thighs - there, that is it darling - now let me lay hold of your dear instrument and guide it into my warm wetness that craves your manliness."

He placed himself on her beautiful smooth and silken body and pressed against the hair of her mound. With her long tapering fingers, she guided him into the opening to the gates of heaven. Aaron trembled in every limb and almost felt sick with excitement - but when he felt the delicious sensation for the first time in years caused by the insertion of his member into the smooth warm oily folds of her mound of desire, he gave but one shove which carried him deep within her so that he actually swooned with delight. He had found heaven.

When he exploded in her, he laid on her, breathing heavily, his member still sheathed into her warmth. Jasmine rhythmically squeezed his love muscle with gyrations inside her opening. Suddenly, he was throbbing in the most ecstatic way as she was pressing and closing with every fold on his swelling member - which had hardly lost any of its pristine stiffness; as his eyes began to discern her features, an exquisite smile played upon his darling lover's lips.

"Old stud," she whispered, "you have given me a torrent of your essence and you are still ready for more. And you are the guy who said your virility had long ago taken flight. Did you like it?"

"Oh my dear, I have never experienced anything so glorious in all my life. I feel like a teenager again. No joy could give me any greater pleasure," he said, but little did he know what followed would make the present interlude pale in comparison.

Aaron began to move gently in and out as she cried, "Oh that is so good baby. Keep that rhythm up, easy now, plunge in a bit deeper with each thrust."

THE GIRL WHO SAID GOODBYE
FOR THE LAST TIME

She moved in unison with him, meeting each slow thrust down by an equal movement upwards, and squeezing his member in the most delicious manner internally.

Oh! He was ecstatic, as his member swollen to its utmost size, seemed to fill her exquisite mound of desire, as she contracted to embrace tightly with its smooth and slippery folds Aaron's throbbing stiffness. Aaron's hands roamed everywhere and his mouth sucked her lips and tongue, or wandered over her pulpy breasts, sucking their tiny nipples. The consciousness almost subsided as Aaron was thrusting his most private part into a sacred delicacy that caused him to experience the most enraptured pleasure. Maddened by the intensity of his feeling, at length he quickened his pace. His charming companion did the same, and together they yielded down a most copious and delicious discharge. Aaron withdrew, and they drifted off to sleep.

It was now perfect sunny daylight, and his enchanting mistress looked so lovely in her almost transparent night-shirt that he was emboldened to ask her to let him see her perfectly naked in all her glorious beauty of form. She gratified him at once, swirling about.

They clasped each other in a most enrapturing embrace, and then Jasmine allowed him to turn her in every direction so as to see, admire, and devour every charm of her exquisitely formed body. Oh! she was indeed beautiful - shoulders broad, and high, and upper neck, flat, not showing any projection of the collar bone; breasts firm, well separated and round, with the most exquisite rosy nipples not much developed; a perfect waist that was naturally indented, with charming swelling hips, and an alluring bottom. Oh, how beautiful her bottom was, making Aaron's heart palpitate with excitement. Then her belly, undulating so enticingly, and swelling out, covered with small crops of silky and curly dark hair; then the entrance to the grotto of love had such delicious pouting lips, rosy, but with hair still thick on each side. Her two alabaster thighs, worthily supported by their large well-rounded fleshy forms made Aaron actually shiver. How beautiful, elegant, and elongated her legs were, rising from well-turned ankles and dainty beautiful feet. Her skin exuded softness, and was dazzlingly fair and smooth. She was a perfect goddess of beauty. In his whole life, Aaron had never seen anything that surpassed her. This divine creature was, when naked, perfect in all her parts as well as beautiful in the face. She was voluptuous by nature, and had a mind that embraced the mysteries of love and lust to display her magnificence. This was woman brought to complete perfection, shaped by the hand of an artist of lust and love.

THE GIRL WHO SAID GOODBYE
FOR THE LAST TIME

They caressed each other with such mutual satisfaction that nature soon drove them to a closer and more active union of the bodies. Fondly embracing one another, they rolled about in the bed and being equally excited, threw themselves into a frenzy, and, in the exquisite contact of naked flesh, enjoyed a long bout of lovemaking, in which Aaron's most charming companion exhibited all the resources of amorous enjoyment. They must have enjoyed the raptures of lovemaking fully half an hour before bringing on the grand finale, in which Jasmine showed extraordinary suppleness of her delicious body by throwing her legs over Aaron's back, pushing her bottom forward with her heels, and raising and sinking her bottom in unison with each thrust of his terribly stiff member, which seemed to swell and become thicker and harder than ever. In retiring from each thrust, her grotto of love seemed to close upon his stiffness with the force of a pair of pincers. They both came to the ecstatic moment at the same time, and both actually screamed with lustful delight.

"Oh, my beloved Aaron," she said, "never, never, have I experienced such pleasure in my entire life."

Smiling, Aaron crept down her body toward the root of her desire and gently blew on it before kissing and finding the root of her passion which he began to manipulate with mouth and fingers, making her rise to meet each motion.

The convulsive twitches of her buttocks, the pressure forward of her hand on his head, all proved the exquisite felicity his lovely paramour was enjoying.

"Oh, my darling Aaron, come up to my arms that I may kiss you for the exquisite delight you have given me." He did so, but took care, in drawing himself up, to gorge his stiffness into her opening and to surrender to passion one more time. Thus passed their first glorious day together. There would be many more.

Exhausted by the numerous encounters he had in love's battlefield, Aaron fell into a deep and sound sleep However, the next morning Aaron sprung up, and in an instant, without a word being said, had her on her back, and was into her delicious opening as far as he could drive his stiff-standing member. His energy and fury seemed to please and stimulate the lady, for she replied to every eager thrust with an eager spring forward. In such haste matters were very speedily brought to a climax with mutual sighs, and "oh's" and "ah's," they sank exhausted, and lay for a very short time. Then, pushing himself down the bed, Aaron applied his lips and tongue to her lovely mound, all wet with discharge, which was so sweet to the taste that he began licking between the lips, and threw her into an ecstasy of delight, until again she had a delicious discharge. Then creeping up, he thrust his member into her well-moistened and velvety opening.

Suddenly, reality returned as Aaron looked up at the dirty ceiling in the dingy hotel room. His mind, flashing a kaleidoscope of memories, had been on a journey to the past where all hope seemed to have died the day Jasmine walked out. It was then that Aaron remembered that he was supposed to be a writer, but how can anyone write without a muse he thought. His muse was gone, and along with her his inspiration. Then, he blinked his eyes and realized where he was. Yes, he was in a dingy hotel room, dying and there was Jasmine by his side again. The room began to swirl about and a golden light seemed to be gleaming from above.

Aaron, who was slipping in and out of consciousness, looked over at the beautiful woman who seemed out of place in all the despair that lay before them. Jasmine was a vision of beauty among the squalor that surrounded them. There was just something unreal and eerie about her. Her face, somewhat luminous, had a dark tone to it. The eyes were a piercingly sharp shade of darkness that mesmerized all who gazed into them. Eyebrows were arched over the curve before dispersing onto the bridge of her nose. Luscious and full, the lips had a provocative pout to them. The enchanting face was framed with slightly wavy, coal dark hair that cascaded over her slightly muscular but incredibly seductive shoulders. Overall, she was truly an unearthly beauty, a magnificent specimen of womanhood that seemed to lure all men who gazed upon her into a prison of desire. This was more than a woman. This was a Goddess!

She was a statuesque woman, who was nearly six feet tall, stood with an air of carefree confidence that was most noticeable in her serene, pouty, mischievous smile that would slowly spread infectiously across her inviting mouth, exposing gleaming white teeth that sparkled in the darkness that surrounded her and Aaron. Her delicately soft face with rounded cheek bones, high trimmed brows and rounded chin was complimented by her easy, charming way that had obviously overwhelmed a plethora of men in her life. Wondrous oceans of playful curiosity were no doubt within that mind that lay beneath what was the most beguiling hair imaginable. It seemed to flutter in a non-existent breeze and its sheen sparkled so brightly that one felt the desire to put sunglasses on to lessen the glare. Being tall, her lithe arms and hands were much longer than normal, but were in perfect symmetry to her flowing magnificent body that captured the attention and manifested the ardour of all lucky enough to gaze upon it. Overall, her general shape was a toned, hourglass figure defining her chest and hips which were of moderate, if not winding definition. Her breasts had perkiness to them as the nipples pierced through the tight-fitting blouse, making men wonder what it would be like to kiss, nibble and suckle on them.

Most men look at women like they were books. If the cover doesn't catch their eye, they will not bother to read what's inside. Ah, but not reading what was inside Jasmine was turning your back on the true beauty of this woman. People are like stained-glass windows. They sparkle and shine when the sun is out, but when the darkness sets in, their true beauty is revealed only if there is a light from within, and Jasmine had that light from within. The light within her was so bright one could almost imagine her being a divinity, all-powerful, all-consuming and all-knowing. Yes, that was it; she was a deity in tight-fitting jeans, body-hugging t-shirt and high heels. Within her dwelled the infinite wisdom of the ages and the sacred creative force that brought light to darkness, hope to despair and love to the loveless.

She was a wild mustang that needed to be a free spirit not corralled and barred from roaming the prairies of euphoric blissfulness that lay like a shining beacon lighting the way to paradise. If not let roam free, a wild mustang will be stifled, trained for subservience and made to wither and grovel before its master, rather than soaring to the heights of glory reserved for the wild and free. Her pounding rapturous huffs stirred up the prairie wind of desire as the dust of euphoria flew about proclaiming her glory. Yes, she was a mustang of avidity that made men's blood boil with erotic cravings. She had left a string of awe-struck wranglers who failed to capture and tame her wild spirit. She was a woman who blazed across the prairies of passion, leaving a wake of yearning among all men who cast a longing eye upon her.

Aaron's mind was racing now as he looked into her eyes and could see the pain on her face. Jasmine must still love him, he thought. Yes, she had left him, but there was still love there. She had found him hadn't she? Yes, in the end, she came to him, came to him in all his despair so that he could breathe his last breath in her presence. His mind was a racing kaleidoscope of the past, as he wondered in and out of consciousness, recalling the events of a life that once had hope and promise but had slipped into a morass of blame and recriminations for that over which he had no control. Aaron' sickness of the mind had brought him to financial and emotional ruin as he lay nearly lifeless in a dingy hotel on Skid Row. Still, among all the squalor, there she was. Yes, he was not poor now. He was he richest man in the world

THE GIRL WHO SAID GOODBYE
FOR THE LAST TIME

as he lay dying, because she was there - Jasmine was there holding his frail hand as he waited for the veil of darkness to finally end his pain.

Blinking his eyes, his mind returned to that time when he and Jasmine met on the streets of Stockholm. Ah, what a glorious event. It was night and it was then that Aaron realized, looking into her dark brown eyes, that he could not reach the dawn but by path of the night. Though her mouth said one thing, her eyes seemed to say, "Do not leave me, for within my heart dwells your future."

At that very moment, on the streets of Stockholm, Aaron realized that he had no past, and he had not future without Jasmine by his side. If he stayed, there was going in his staying; and if he went, there was staying in his going. How could he lose faith now that the path to rapturous contentment lay before him. He did not know it, of course, but this was the beginning of pain.

Aaron that night reflected on a Gibranian anecdote of the true mark of a woman's depth of character. He began that night to despise his soul for not being more like Jasmine. She was the type of woman who would limp when among the crippled to fit in and share their pain. She would be meeker when among the meekest. When choosing between the hard and easy, she always chose the hard to prove she could endure. When committing a wrong she always made amends with contriteness. When seeing the weaknesses of others, she professed to be weaker still. She only spoke of virtue and praised those who received none. She was humble and pleaded ignorance, rather than intelligence. Her gratuitous gestures of kindness were the sparkle and the twinkle on the brightest stars in heaven.

The space between Aaron's imagination and his attainment could only be traversed by his longing for this woman who had captured his heart that night in Stockholm. Aaron had picked up the key to paradise that night, but over the years he had lost it somewhere between sanity of purpose and insanity of actions. His was a lonely journey into the deepest reaches of that which imprisoned him without him even knowing that he was shackled and chained to the machinations of psychological and emotional turmoil that boiled in his mind like a caldron of hot oil. The mind can be a dark place that traps a man in his own deception.

The ecstasy of their courtship was interrupted by Jasmine's brief sojourn in North Africa, where she hid out from the CIA to not only save her life, but to protect Aaron from harm, but fate would bring her and Aaron together again and their lives would traverse through the corridors of mystery and intrigue, making their journeys a cacophony of adventure and excitement.

THE GIRL WHO SAID GOODBYE
FOR THE LAST TIME

Ah, and the sex. The glorious sex! Oh, the fornication was a non-stop. After work, whenever Aaron walked through the door, there would be Jasmine, sprawled across the arm of the sofa, her ass jutting up into the air, wiggling and squirming in anticipation of Aaron's rear entry welcome home. He would quickly remove his clothes as he stared at the delight awaiting him. He stood less than a metre from the large hole facing him as he was stroking himself. It only took about five seconds before his fingers were gently touching her bare skin. Rubbing and lightly caressing her soft butt, he bent over and kissed her cheeks. At first, he stood still and let her gently rub back against him, using her crack to arouse him as he placed his throbbing member between her cheeks. His touching got firmer but in a warm, sensual way. Jasmine could feel the heat of his passion emanating from his touch. He gradually started to run his fingers on the top part of her ass crack, then gently slid them in under his tool of delight, looking for that magic spot that always made her sigh in anticipation of the plunge into her hole of pleasure.

To make it easier for him, she completely relaxed her muscles, giving him easier access to that which he so longingly desired. Slowly, but gently he pushed only slightly inside her as the head of his member became saturated with the KY jelly she had placed in the opening.

THE GIRL WHO SAID GOODBYE
FOR THE LAST TIME

Her mind was prodigiously racing and hoping for complete and total immersion into pleasure, so she bent over a little more and backed all the way to meet his slow thrust. Finally it happened; he had entered her tightness and was preparing for the final thrust that would put him into the chamber of ecstasy.

Aaron went slowly at first, only going in a little at a time. Gradually he entered her fully and began pumping. The pumping was at a slow even pace that was working nicely for her as she sighed and moaned. Aaron placed his hand on her leg and started manipulating her opening on the other side. He took the liberty of grabbing his member and began alternating between the openings to paradise. First working one hole, pulling it out and then plunging into the other hole. So lose was she that he lost track of which hole he was in. Oh, the pleasure – the pleasure.

Jasmine drifted into total euphoria only to be brought back to reality each time he pulled out of one hole to enter the other. The pounding continued for what seemed hours as both lovers were in complete blissfulness. Jasmine felt as if she was a prisoner of desire. Oh, but it was a prison of her own making, and she wanted to stay in it, never being let free of the exquisite delight that was bringing her so much pleasure. Suddenly, Aaron exploded in her back cavity like a volcano erupting in a frenzy dumping the debris from the explosion deep inside her.

Neither lover had uttered a word. Aaron pulled out and moved backward toward the wall by the front door, his member at half staff now. He was breathing heavily and could not help but smile when Jasmine arose and a bit of white liquid oozed out from between her cheeks and dribbled down her left leg. She turned and moved toward Aaron slowly, not looking at him, but looking down at what was between his legs as she licked her lips provocatively. She dropped to her knees about a metre from Aaron and crawled the rest of the way until she was right in front of the object that was the focus of her desire. The object began to rise as she slowly opened her mouth. She only blew on it and began to fondle it. She slowly licked and kissed it, gradually taking it into her mouth. Since it was not fully erect, she worked furiously to make it more to her liking. Bringing it down her throat as far as it would go, in few seconds it became an ever hardening dynamo of pleasure. She began to move slow, then fast – all the way in, then almost out before plunging her mouth deep on it again.

Finally she felt the beginning of the pulsating that meant the flow of white gooey stuff that she craved was on its way up the shaft to pound against the back of her throat and trickle down into her. Aaron let out a loud sigh and she gobbled it all up with the fervour of someone who had not had a drink of water in days.

All that was the glorious past when the two of them had always been in a sexual frenzy, but Aaron was 82 now, and as Jasmine sat there holding his hand, a tear formed in her eye as she looked at the man who had been her salvation at a time when she was floundering in a stormy sea of lost hope. He had reached down and plucked her from the storm and brought her to safe harbour in his arms.

Aaron was drifting precariously in and out of consciousness, as Jasmine and he were only waiting now in the dingy hotel room for the blissful end to a man who had been on a steady journey the past couple of years into an abyss of hopelessness. Aaron, unable to talk, stared at the ceiling, and then turned his eyes toward his blessed Jasmine who gave off a celestial glow. It was then that she let a little smile creep across her lips. Aaron blinked his eyes and drifted off into memories of his deteriorating fall into misery after picking up the envelope.

When he first arrived at the flophouse, he took a walk every night and he always noticed a lady, dressed in black, standing under the light-post exactly opposite the door into the shelter. She always turned her face towards him and followed him with her eyes when he passed by her.

Aaron looked out of the corner of his eye and realized she always had the same dress on, always the same veil that concealed most of her face and fell over her breasts, and that she carried in her hand a small umbrella with an ivory ring in the handle. It was the third evening he had seen her there, always in the same place. As soon as he passed by her, she turned slowly and went down the street away from him. His nervous brain vibrated with curiosity. As after all, he was still Aaron Adams, Private Eye, and he became at once possessed by the unreasonable feeling that he was the object of her visit. At last he was almost on the point of addressing her, of asking her if she was looking for anyone, if she needed his assistance in any way, or if he might accompany her home to assure her safety on the bad streets that were typical of American neighbourhoods where the poor, the downtrodden and the forgotten are cast aside by an uncaring society. Shabbily dressed, as Aaron unfortunately was, he might protect her through the dark streets; but he had an undefined fear that it perhaps might cost him something more than he was willing to pay.

His distressingly empty pockets acted in a far too depressing way upon him, and he had not even the courage to scrutinize her sharply as he passed her by. Hunger had once more taken up its abode in his breast, and he had not tasted food since the evening before. Added to this was the fact that he lay and shivered all night, lay fully dressed as he stood and walked in the daytime, lay blue with cold, lay and froze every night with fits of icy shivering, and grew stiff during his sleep.

He went down the street to think over what he had to do to keep alive until he figured out a way to survive another day. Then again, maybe it would be better if he did not survive. What was the use? There was nothing for him now that Jasmine had deserted him.

He went into Hooper's Cafe and passed a dozen tables at which men sat chatting, eating, and drinking. He went into the back of the café until he was grabbed by the shoulders and told to leave, because he was an affront to dignity. In the past, Aaron would have stood his ground and let the man have an earful of just what he thought of the arrogance of those who judged others by their dress and their economic status.

Crestfallen and annoyed, he dragged himself out again into the street. Wasn't it now the very hottest eternal devil existing to think that his hardships never would come to an end! Only death would end those. Taking long furious strides, with the collar of his coat hunched savagely up round his ears, and his hands thrust in his pockets, he strode along, cursing his fate along the way. Not one real untroubled hour, not the common food necessary to hold body and soul together seemed possible for a man who once was considered moderately wealthy. He laughed sarcastically at his delicate rectitude, spat contemptuously in the street, and could not find words half strong enough to mock himself for his stupidity. He had suffered so unspeakably that he was prepared to do anything. Well, anything but go back home and see a home empty of Jasmine and empty of hope, empty of the love he craved so desperately. His was a solitary journey into despair.

It was around eleven. The streets were fairly dark, and the people roamed about in all directions, quiet pairs and noisy groups mixed with one another. The great hour of ineptitude of purpose had commenced, the pairing time when the mystic traffic is in full swing and the hour of merry adventures sets in. Rustling about the street were couples ending their evening, sensual laughter, heaving bosoms, passionate, panting breaths, and far down near the Bowery Hotel, a voice could be heard shouting, "repent, repent while there is time." The whole street was a teaming mass of men and women in search of a meaning to that for which there was no meaning. Life is just life thought Aaron, nothing more nothing less.

THE GIRL WHO SAID GOODBYE
FOR THE LAST TIME

He felt involuntarily in his pockets for money that was not there. The passion that thrills through the movements of every one of the passers-by, the dim light of the streetlamps, the quiet dark night, all commenced to affect him. The air was laden with whispers, embraces, trembling admissions, concessions, half-uttered words and suppressed cries. A number of cats were declaring their love with loud yells in the alleyways. Yes, thought Aaron, the squeals of passion that denotes love.

Aaron's misery and wretchedness of spirit soon overwhelmed him. What utter humiliation and disgrace it was to sink so low he thought. Yet, he no longer cared, because he no longer possessed any pride.

In order to consol himself, he took to picking all possible faults in the people who glided by. He shrugged his shoulders contemptuously, and looked dismissively at them as they passed. People seeking happiness were all about, looking for that which was in their own backyard, but they were too stupid to see it. Maybe coming to mingle with the poor was a way of coping – a way to convince themselves that there were others worse off than they were. Ah, and the street whores roamed about in short dresses, low-cut tops and five inch heels upon which they precariously balanced themselves with a swaggering contemptible attitude of not giving a damn about themselves or those to whom they offered their services. Theirs was a lonely profession on the fringes of hopelessness.

Then Aaron thought of his profession, private investigator. It was even lonelier than that of a street prostitute. You could trust no one. You saw only the seedy side of life, and dealt with those who had no virtue and no honour. You saw the basest of human emotions and had to constantly confront schemers, whose sole aim was to cheat, defraud, steal and swindle people of their dignity. The selfishness and cowardliness of people who had no principles was evident in the individuals with whom Aaron came into contact more often than not. Ah, and then there were the murderers – those we had no conscience and no remorse for taking a human life. They were plotting schemers against conscience of thought and deed. Remorse and recompense was simply not part of their vocabulary of deceit. Perhaps, thought Aaron, that explained his constant depression. His profession was like an anvil of pain that pulled him into a pit of despair.

Aaron always had to struggle to keep from being overwhelmed by the world around him. It was a world not to his liking. One that he strived to change, but the forces arrayed against him were too powerful and too entrenched to be moved. Each individual was for sale, and had their price. Most times, the price was cheap. However, Aaron

THE GIRL WHO SAID GOODBYE
FOR THE LAST TIME

had no for sale sign on his soul. His integrity, his honour and his principled rectitude were not for sale at any price.

As he meandered down a street of lost hope in a part of town filled with people trapped in a downward spiral of misery, he found himself thinking of the woman with an umbrella whose face was covered with a veil. Who was she? Why was she there on the street corner every night? His mind was racing now for memories lost in the sands of time. Did he know her? Suddenly he had a Cashian moment of reflection and recalled a poem that he altered to fit the situation. A situation that was slowly crystallizing itself in his mind. Yes, he knew the woman was looking for him.

Many years ago on a cold dark night
she was slain near the homeless shelter lamp light.
All those present turned their backs,
and did not care about the cold hard facts.
She walks the streets in a long black veil,
She visits the crime scene as the night winds wail,
Nobody knows, nobody cares but her.

The policeman said "everyone has an alibi."
He shrugged his shoulders and let out a sigh.
She was a just a streetwalker and no one cared.

J. Wayne Frye

THE GIRL WHO SAID GOODBYE
FOR THE LAST TIME

It was the devil they all feared.
Oh, she walks these streets in a long black veil.
She visits the crime scene as the night winds wail.

Nobody knows, nobody cares but her.
Death smiled and told her the living did not care.
She walked into eternity and no one shed a tear.
Now, at night when the cold winds blow,
In a long black veil she refuses to let injustice go.
Oh, she walks these streets in a long black veil.
She visits the crime scene as the night winds wail.
Nobody knows, nobody cares but her.

J. Wayne Frye   125

THE GIRL WHO SAID GOODBYE
FOR THE LAST TIME

CHAPTER 7
NOTHING MORE THAN A CAPITALIST

You murdered me.
Murdered me for what you thought was love.
Murder that was covered up with unmitigated lies.
You committed murder as I looked into your eyes.

Aaron turned and started walking back to the shelter. Yes, the woman was there for a reason. She must have been looking for him, but how did she find him? How did she locate a down and out private eye in the Bowery?

Aaron's spirits began to soar just a bit. He was living on Skid Row with the rest of the bums, living with people lost in a downward spiral of hopelessness. But even down in the Bowery, even as an old man, Aaron was still the best damn private eye in New York.

As Aaron approached the lamppost, there she was. Despite the veil, you knew that under it was an extraordinarily beautiful woman. You could tell her figure was magnificently formed with curves in all the right places. She was slightly plump, but in a sensual way. As she stared off into the fog, Aaron moved toward her gingerly, not wanting to frighten her. Slowly she turned her head toward Aaron and he froze. Through the veil, one could still see the almost radiant dark piercing eyes.

THE GIRL WHO SAID GOODBYE
FOR THE LAST TIME

She said nothing as Aaron slowly strode toward her, his shoulders stooped and his eyes focused on her veil. There was a transparent misty vapour forming at her feet and you could hear a faint moan, a whining that was so forlorn it cut to the bone. She was weeping.

Lamppost where the strange woman was standing when Aaron Adams returned to the shelter to confront her. The eerie light from the nearby lamp cast a ghostly glow all about her, and a misty vapour seemed to slowly rise from the sidewalk. This was the beginning of one of Aaron's strangest adventures.

THE GIRL WHO SAID GOODBYE
FOR THE LAST TIME

Aaron reached out with his right hand and touched her on the left arm to let her know he cared. He could feel how cold she was even through her coat sleeve. Yet, she was not shaking at all. Her deportment was one of almost ghostly proportions.

Standing there in his threadbare clothing, his hair dishevelled, breathing heavily and emaciated, Aaron was not the dashing, distinguished older gentleman he once was just a short time ago. He was nothing but a Bowery bum now, but that did not seem to matter to the young woman who was weeping. She looked up and through the veil, as her eyes seemed to glow a crimson red, in a faint whisper she said, "I could not approach you. I had to wait for you to approach me, Mr. Adams. You must help someone who is desperate. You can free this person from a prison of turmoil that will keep the gates of heaven closed until the truth comes out. She is a desperate woman."

Aaron looked into those penetrating eyes and said, "You know me, but I do not know you. How did you find me? No one knows where I am." At the final word he looked down at the side walk and the misty vapour was now up to her knees. She seemed to be unsteady, swaying back and forth just a bit as she said. "Who I am is not important. How I found you is unimportant. I am here, because I need a private detective to ferret out a killer. You are my last hope. Mr. Adams, please find the killer and bring justice that has been denied."

Aaron, his curiosity aroused, said, "And just who was killed?"

The lady, almost in a whisper replied, "Clarisse Coleman. She was just a woman forced to prostitute herself in order to survive in a country with no heart and no compassion."

Aaron wanted to tell her that he was no longer up to the job, but he decided that he would make one last attempt at being a private eye. He was dying of misery and loneliness, and this might just be what he needed to get his heart beating again.

He sighed, and the vapour was now up to her waist and ever so slowly creeping further up. She took a deep breath and pointed at the clock on the corner.

It was then, as he looked at the clock that the darkness seemed to claim him; the unfathomable black eternity surrounded him. He had never seen a night so black. How dark it was! He thought of dark monsters waiting to devour him and chew on his soul. He wanted to cry out in terror, as he clasped his hands together, rubbing them furiously, frightened like a little child confounded with nightmarish dreams. He glimpsed upwards again and slowly turned to face the woman. He was feeling fear through every pore in his body as the lamp twinkled and fizzled. He felt relief that the darkness was apparently fading. Then, a pall of doom descended upon Aaron as he gazed up at the sky and thought it was no ordinary sky. The darkness was slowly moving down toward him, ready to crush him. No, it was not the sky; it was the lid slowly closing on his coffin. The darkness trapped him in terror. He had not known terror like this, since he was in the jungles of Vietnam trying to survive.

Finally, Aaron turned all the way around. The woman was gone, seemingly vanishing into thin air. He looked down the alley a few feet away and saw that mysterious vapour moving through the alleyway. He actually shivered, wondering what was amiss. Yet, he was Aaron Adams, and that meant something in New York City. He had been wandering the streets now for nearly two years, and the time had come for him to one last time throw off the misery briefly, so he might solve a crime. Yes, Aaron Adams was back in business.

So, Aaron was now ready to do the woman's bidding. A fee had not been discussed. "Ah." He whispered to himself. "I did not even ask for a retainer. Damn, I could have got my hands on a few dollars."

THE GIRL WHO SAID GOODBYE
FOR THE LAST TIME

He strolled up the street and coming toward him was an extraordinarily beautiful woman taking long smooth strides that reminded him of a gazelle loping across the plains of Africa. Her size was medium, her figure beautifully formed, her face handsome and expressive, her eyes keen, yet mild, her breasts perfectly formed like cantaloupes, her stride soft and confident.

Aaron lifted his weary head, and felt deep within the glorious blessing of renewed confidence. The woman who looked fixedly at him as he came closer to her, said, "Good evening Mr. Adams."

Hum, Aaron thought. Why was she out walking so late? Did not a young beautiful lady run a risk being in Bowery at that time of night? And how did she know him? There was something strange going on, two women who knew him and he knew neither one. She stared at him with astonishment, scanned his face closely, turned to face the same direction that Aaron was going, then thrust her hand suddenly under his arm, and said, "You don't know me any more than you knew the other woman you met tonight, but old man, you are about to take a trip into the twilight zone. I am going to be your guide."

What follows is as accurate a retelling as possible of Aaron's journey that night. There are some who will confuse it with Dante's Inferno, and most will claim it was nothing more than a figment of an old, morose man's imagination. It has been passed on to me through several sources, so to its accuracy I cannot attest. For those who believe in spirits, heaven and hell, it will be a splendid rendering in support of those beliefs. I shall let my readers be the judge of what they want to believe and disbelieve.

The lady led Aaron toward a dark tunnel at the end of the sidewalk. It simply appeared out of nowhere. It was like a black hole, seemingly sucking them in with great ferocity. Aaron, not caring whether he lived or died for over two years, had no fear. With the woman by his side, the giant tunnel just opened up and swallowed them in the darkness of eternity. Yes, Aaron thought he was dead. But he was not destined for a heaven in which he did not believe. This tunnel led to hell.

As they cascaded down what seemed an endless hole of darkness, Aaron thought back on his life, and especially his career as a writer the past few years as he had let his detective business flounder while pursuing that which he thought offered a better opportunity to reach out to people and give them hope. It also got him out of the muck, despair and hopelessness that had become his lot in life as a detective, because he was only exposed to the worst in people in what many looked upon as a dirty rotten business conducted by dirty rotten men.

Aaron's penchant for writing had led to some modest success, but he had been told by Jasmine, rather disdainfully, that he was retreating to a fantasy land of unreality to escape from life. Yet, Aaron refused to accept her analysis, because he asked himself where the world would be without dreamers. There would be no music, no great literature, no classic films, no great works of art, and what about the great discoveries of science? Were not all those people avid dreamers? If Jonas Salk had not dreamed of a cure for polio, how many people would still be afflicted? Had those who dreamed of the computer been passed off as fools in search of fantastical escapism, the world would not have the miracle of instant communication that knows no distance too great. Well, Aaron dreamed that one of his books might create the next revolutionary like Che Guevara who would arouse a passion for justice among the masses and foment a rebellion that would lift mankind out of bondage. Was not Aaron's flight into unreality a tool that allowed him to have purpose? That which gives meaning to a person's life should never be denigrated. Because of his father, Aaron had always worn heavy scars of ridicule like an anvil that weighs upon the mind and traps a person with feelings of uselessness. Aaron knew deep inside he had a soft heart and was a good and decent person, who saw wrong and tried to right it, who saw suffering and tried to alleviate it, who saw injustice and longed to correct it. Aaron felt if he could only reach one person and move them to take action against injustice and lift just one individual from despair, all his efforts would have accomplished something valuable.

Those thoughts were rushing through Aaron's mind as he continued to be propelled forward through the intense darkness as his guide held tightly to his hand. Aaron was an avowed non-believer, but he knew he was moving ever forward toward hell. Yes, he knew there was no heaven, but he said to himself, "I am about to find out there is a hell."

Suddenly, a giant pit appeared in the distance. He and his guide tumbled into it and seemed to be gently floating downward, almost like an autumn leaf floating ever so slowly toward the ground. They landed on their feet in what appeared to be a dark, savage, rough forest of black trees that were massive burned out hulks with burned cinders piled around the trunks.

In the distance was a black mountain with a flat peak. His guide pulled his hand and they moved forward toward it. The mountain began to undulate and seemed to be gradually moving toward them, shortening the distance they had to travel considerably. A slight rumble, maybe thunder, could be heard from behind the mountain.

Aaron's guide said not a word. She just kept pulling him forward toward the base of the mountain. From the ground began to rise steam and the heat became intense, almost stifling. And the smell, the smell penetrated Aaron's nostrils and almost sickened him. Something was burning, something hideous. Aaron had smelled it before. Yes, he had smelled it in Vietnam after napalm had been dropped. It was burning flesh. The brass had always said it was the smell of victory, but what Aaron smelt there and now here was not victory. It was defeat - the defeat of those who had led lives of evil. The evil of the USA trying to impose its will on a country fighting for freedom had been defeated by the righteous in Viet Nam. Now, the devil was punishing those who had tried to impose their will on the poor and the downtrodden in a cruel economic system, based on greed. He saw those people at the base of the mountain. They were trudging up the mountain dressed in expensive suits and designer dresses that were wrinkled from the heat and covered with soot from the burning cinders. As they neared the base of the mountain, Aaron heard the thunder rumbling above the mountain now, but there was no lightning. Aaron remembered his science lesson – there can be no thunder without lightning.

THE GIRL WHO SAID GOODBYE
FOR THE LAST TIME

Yet, there was none above the mountain, only the deathly roar of clamouring thunder that seemed to be violently shaking the peak of the mountain as the people beside Aaron and his guide moved ever upward.

As Aaron and his guide moved ever closer to the top of the mountain, Aaron's mind could not fathom what was happening. Then the thunder roared again, and he realized that it was not thunder at all. No, it was the clamouring voices of what seemed like millions coming from the other side of the mountain. Oh, but what piteous wails. There was a pleading in the voices, a solicitation for compassion. But in this evil place there was no compassion, no hope and no way out.

As Aaron made his way up the mountain, he removed the worn, flayed picture of Jasmine from his breast pocket and staring at it for a second before putting it back in his pocket, he recalled all he and Jasmine had shared over the years, and he could not understand how she could so cavalierly discard him. However, he did know that by now she had probably given her heart to another man and was never going to embrace him again. Still, he pined for her day and night. He was just an old man now who was walking the streets, staying in shelters, gasping for breath in a world that had collapsed around him. He recalled what he had once told Jasmine when she was despondent about her lot in life: *underestimating your worth allows others to ignore your value.*

Aaron was a realist, and he knew that he had actually over estimated his value to Jasmine. He had made assumptions that were erroneous at their core. She was, after all, a woman who needed love and felt she was not getting it from Aaron. He knew that by now, nearly two years later, she had sought the arms of another to seek solace from that which she saw as putting her on a precipice that opened into a dark pit of mental anguish that had already devoured Aaron. She, no doubt, was now being unwittingly mesmerized by a man who had no core, but offered the superficial manifestations of what she thought was actual love. His control of her would be complete, and she would willingly submit to his will, confusing the urge to control her every move with devotion and love rather than infatuated self-gratifying egomania.

Aaron thought that a relationship was placing one's heart & soul in the hands of another while taking responsibility for another in ones own heart & soul. He thought providing Jasmine security excused his sometimes abysmal behaviour that weighed so heavily on her mind. In his heart, he believed he was showing Jasmine true love and devotion, but now that it was too late, he realized that his total descent into mental anguish was destroying that which he treasured more than his own life. He wanted to plead with her to look inside him, to see the true depth of his love, rather than only observing the illness that made him a pariah to her. But by now, all her love would have been transferred to another man whom she thought was superior in every way to Aaron. Aaron was no longer able to reach her. He could never rekindle that which once meant so much to her. She could not accept the fact that Aaron was mere flesh & bones, with scars, feelings, thoughts & ideals.

When we enter the world of another being we must be willing to be a part of it all. When someone entrusts their heart to you, they are giving you a piece of their soul. You cannot treat a soul casually. You must protect, nurture and handle it with care. Aaron's soul had been tossed into the trash heap of lost hope.

As his tour guide through the hell before him led him up the mountain of darkness, he turned his head back, looking over his shoulder, trying to see the opening to the tunnel of despair that had devoured him, but the opening was closed. All hope was lost.

Aaron looked at his guide and began to see her as the Medusa. Her eyes were turning a fierce red and her long hair seemed to be slowly tangling into long braids that appeared to be like snakes undulating across the ground. The veins in her neck began to pulsate and tremble. He wanted to plead with her to take another road to hell, a road filled with less suffering. Surely, there must be a less savage route thought Aaron.

At first he had thought his guide was beautiful, but as they ascended the mountain with the other lost souls, she became more and more hideous looking. She appeared malignant and ruthless. Everything about her appearance appeared to be the opposite of love and virtue.

The closer they got to the peak, the more desperate were the lamentations of the lost souls toiling in eternal fire on the other side. Aaron began to ask himself if he was a believer would he now be ascending to heaven rather than trudging up a mountain of burning cinders to a black peak that was belching fire. He knew what waited on the other side. Yes, he knew that once you reached the peak that there would then be a descent into the eternal fires of hell. There was a vile, disgusting smell of burning flesh penetrating his nostrils that nearly made him regurgitate, as he caught the vomit half way up his oesophagus.

In this kingdom of fire and pain, there was one who ruled supreme, but there were lesser devils who now were coming into view. At the top of the hill were fire breathing demons with red penetrating eyes, flapping skeletal wings and large ram like horns emanating from their large heads. From their mouths came putrid, nearly overpowering smells that seemed to be whisked forward by a swirling wind. The wings were transparent and making an eerie noise as they flapped.

The agony before Aaron made him have hope that maybe there was punishment, even eternal damnation, for those who practiced heartless domination of others. Had these souls writhing in pain been the captains of industry who brutalized workers and got rich on the backs of their labour? Were these tormented beings former government officials and elected representatives who had practiced ruthless disregard for those they were supposed to serve while only serving their own interests? Were these the souls of those who practiced torture in the name of patriotism? Were these souls the remnants of pontificators of deceit who used religion to point the finger of condemnation? Ah, thought Aaron, perhaps hell is a just destination for those who practiced hypocritical arrogance.

The lady who had his hand looked him in the eyes and said, "She who wears the black veil is in torment, because the one who causes her suffering is not here, serving his sentence in hell. Bring him to justice, Mr. Adams. Bring him here."

THE GIRL WHO SAID GOODBYE
FOR THE LAST TIME

Aaron blinked his eyes for a split second and when he opened them, he was standing on the street corner by the lamp where he had seen the lady. Taking a deep breathe he realized he had been hallucinating. His mind was on such a downward spiral that his descent into madness was nearly complete. It seemed so real. Then he had second thoughts when he turned and there she was by the lamppost again – the lady in the black veil.

Confounded and confused all Aaron could mutter was, "you, you want me to do something for you? However, I am not sure I am up to the task any longer. You can see that I am a mental and physical wreck of a man. Surely you can find someone better suited to the task than a worn-out, destitute old man."

The lady, softly, almost in a dreamlike voice said, "I know you and your reputation. You may be old. You may appear worn out, but within you still beats the heart of a champion. You are a man who seeks justice, honours truth and fights against a system that offers no hope. That is why I seek you out Mr. Adams. You are a man who deplores an unjust world, a man who refuses to bend before the winds of adversity. You are the one man who can rectify a wrong and bring justice that has been denied for far too long. You sir are the last hope for the hopeless."

THE GIRL WHO SAID GOODBYE
FOR THE LAST TIME

Aaron, looking into her hollow, piercing eyes said, "You want me to find Clarisse Colman's killer?"

"I do Mr. Adams. Seek and you shall find it is said. You seek justification for an existence that you now think has no meaning, but by finding Clarisse Colman's killer, you will bring meaning back into your life. You are battling the demons of despair, but by doing this task; you can keep those demons at bay for awhile. Do this thing for me, for Clarisse, for yourself."

Aaron, feeling a surge of exhilaration, said "I will do it, but I could use some monetary assistance right now to help me get through the next few days. Could you provide a small retainer?"

"Mr. Adams, I am more destitute than you. All I have is undying gratitude for your help. Beyond that I can offer nothing."

Aaron, accustomed to helping the downtrodden when he was better off financially, could only mutter, "OK, I shall do the best I can for you. Can you tell me where Clarisse lived?"

A tone of appreciation in her voice, the woman replied as she pointed down the street, "118 Carlton, right around the corner."

THE GIRL WHO SAID GOODBYE
FOR THE LAST TIME

Aaron, actually beginning to feel useful, said, "And by what name shall I call you? Where shall I find you if I need you?"

The woman, almost in a whisper, replied, "I'll find you." She then turned and walked toward the nearby alley, never looking back as Aaron stood there dumbfounded, but determined to once again pursue justice in a land where it was far too often nothing more than an illusion.

Determined to make the best of things, Aaron was about to head toward the hotel, take a shower, change clothes and finally get back to living. However, a burly, stern looking cop, who like most authority figures, appear to enjoy harassing those misfortunate enough to be down and out, strolled Aaron's way with his menacing-looking nightstick swinging in his hand like it was his ticket to arrogant disregard for anyone's rights. Pointing the end of the stick at Aaron's stomach, he said, "Better be moving on old man. You are too old for mischief. Find yourself a doorway and get to sleep."

Aaron, feeling his old bravado said, "Asshole, I am up to no mischief, and I don't need a representative of the authoritarian class to tell me where to bed down for the night. Take a flying fucking leap into the East River where a lot of New York's garbage winds up."

THE GIRL WHO SAID GOODBYE
FOR THE LAST TIME

A look of surprise on his face, the cop[replied, "Listen buddy, don't fuck with New York's finest."

Aaron, a man who always thought that cops were nothing more than licensed thugs for the moneyed class, said, "Finest my ass. I have been here for nearly 50 years and the finest thing I have ever seen any of you do is go on strike. That way, the poor get a few days respite from your harassment. Leave me the fuck alone or you'll spend the rest of the night picking up your teeth off the sidewalk. I'll shove that goddamn night stick so far up your ass it'll tickle your throat!"

The cop, taken aback by the boldness of such an old man, said "Who the hell you think you are buddy?"

Aaron, feeling that old pride swell up inside said, "I am Aaron Adams, and I have never been afraid of you arrogant representatives of the rich and powerful."

The cop, almost trembling at the mention of Aaron Adams, who had often brought down crooked cops over the years, said, "He's dead. Disappeared over two years ago, thank God. Best damn thing that ever happened to this city, getting rid of a troublemaker like him. Stop trying to resurrect the dead old man. Move on – move on."

THE GIRL WHO SAID GOODBYE
FOR THE LAST TIME

Aaron scoffed at him with disdain, shrugged his shoulders and said, "Ever hear of Clarisse Coleman?"

A look of recognition on his face, the cop replied, "Sure, a street walking hussy who got bumped right here on this street. Probably one of her johns she stole money from decided to get even."

Aaron, ever resentful of the disregard displayed for those who lived on the margins of society said, "A prostitute at least brings a little happiness to lonely people rather than looking for someone to club with a nightstick. Hey, at least they are honest about what they do. Policemen prostitute themselves every day by selling out to the rich and powerful while keeping the rest of us in line. You use a nightstick on the poor, but if you arrest a guy from Wall Street, you just ask him to show up at the station with his high-priced attorney, turn himself in and show up to pay his fine, if there is one, while the poor are carted off to the slammer."

The cop snarled, "Buddy, I had enough of your lip for one night." He then pointed up the street with his nightstick and continued, "Move on old dude."

Aaron barked back, "Moving, but not moving on. I am moving forward against injustice."

THE GIRL WHO SAID GOODBYE
FOR THE LAST TIME

Repulsive are the vileness and insidiousness
That emanates from liars' tongues.
There is no humbleness from the exalted,
Who care not for those in quiet desperation.

Among the desperate is resurrected a champion.
He boils with indignation at injustice.
He sees the wickedness of those
Who hurt innocence and destroy compassion.

Voices that mock fairness know no tears,
As the turmoil blots out the sun.
Yet, Aaron Adams carries the sword
Of the executioner held high with honour.

The kingdom of the rich laughs at justice.
Yet, Aaron shall not falter.
He will not succumb to any assault
From the deceitful opposition.

Time shall never break his will,
His momentum or his motivation.
He stares injustice in the face
And does not cower in fear.

Be warned evil enemies of justice!
Ye shall all be judged
And shall quiver under the wake
Of his glorious retribution.

Aaron was now an avenging angel!!! Renewed

J. Wayne Frye

with a vigorous inclination for justice, he had to fight his depression and ride astride that blackest of the horses that galloped down from Apocalypse. Yes, like the Aaron of old, he was about to meat out justice to those who thought they had escaped retribution.

The cold began to get too intense for Aaron to keep still. He moved steadily forward until he arrived at the hotel. It was cold up in his room, and he could barely see the window for the intense darkness around him, but he did not want to disturb his roommate. He felt his way towards the bed, pulled off his shoes, and set about warming his feet by rubbing them with his equally cold hands. Fruitless effort he thought.

Then he lay down with all his clothes on. The following morning he sat up in bed as soon as it got light, removed his dishevelled clothes and pulled some fresh ones from the suitcase by his bed, headed to the washroom at the end of the hall, shaved, showered and got ready to tackle what he knew would be his last case.

Aaron looked out his window. It was snowing. He bustled about the room, took aimless turns to and fro, scratched his head and listened attentively for that little voice within as he quietly and pensively waited for inspiration that would be his guide.

THE GIRL WHO SAID GOODBYE
FOR THE LAST TIME

He thought for a split second that he was mad. Why had he agreed to take the case? After a long time, perhaps a couple of minutes, he pulled himself sharply together and realized that there must be an end to the irrelative pursuit of insanity he thought. He had a case. He had a reason to live

Time went; he heard the traffic in the street, the rattle of cars and the incessant chattering. He meandered down the hotel stairs and into the street as the morning sun tried unsuccessfully to peek through the clouds. He grew weary, and started breathing heavily. He tried afresh to shake himself out of the daze that enveloped him in a mist of thought. His eyes filled with tears. He cried softly to himself. The gloom grew and slowly overwhelmed him. Thoughts came and went as usual, but he kept telling himself that he had a purpose. He was on a case!

He was not hungry anymore, as he realized that it had been so long since he had sustenance that the very thought of food was itself nauseating. His body was withering away little by little. He was gradually disappearing. Yes, he was slowly dissipating into nothingness, slowly but surely.

He found Clarisse's address and knocked on the door. A woman standing in the adjacent doorway said, "Can I help you mister? Ain't been nobody lived there for about a month. Last tenant left in the middle of the night screaming something about a ghost. Longest anybody been able to stay since Clarisse was killed was maybe two months. They is some strange going ons in that there apartment."

Aaron, fascinated, but a stern nonbeliever in the supernatural, replied, "So, you knew Clarisse Coleman?"

"I did indeed. Finest woman I ever knowed. Them who pointed the finger of condemnation at her just ain't able to see the good in people. They only want to see bad. Just cause she sold her body to make ends meet don't mean she can't be a good woman."

Aaron, sensing a fellow sojourner on the road to acceptance rather than condemnation, said, "Ma'am, you seem like a woman who can see beneath the surface of things. I agree with you. Judging people without really knowing them is inappropriate. That old saying 'walk a mile in my shoes should always be heeded."

Smiling through rotted teeth, the woman replied, "Yeah, you got that right mister. Right indeed."

"So," said Aaron as he walked toward her, "you knew her well I take it?"

"I did indeed."

THE GIRL WHO SAID GOODBYE
FOR THE LAST TIME

Aaron, with a serious tone, continued, "I am looking into her death. Seems the authorities were not too concerned about finding the killer."

Shaking her head, the woman said, "Of course not. She was poor. She was a prostitute. Just another one of the throwaways who don't mean nothing to nobody. Well, she meant something to me, and a lotta others too, but we'uns don't count cause we all are throwaways too."

Aaron, feeling the surge of that old indignation for the unjustness of the world, said, "Well, you mean something to me Ma'am. People like you are the ones who really count in my book, not the Park Avenue aristocrats who roll up the windows in their chauffeured limousines to keep from seeing what their greed causes. People like Clarisse might be selling their bodies, but they aren't selling their souls for a hand full of silver."

The old woman let out a laugh and said, "Damn, you my kind a man. You an old gentleman who really knows what's what."

Aaron, smiling, said "So, did Clarisse entertain a lot of gentleman in her apartment? "

Smiling, the old lady said, "Yeah, I must admit to getting a little joy outta hearing the moaning, groaning and the bed shaking."

THE GIRL WHO SAID GOODBYE
FOR THE LAST TIME

Aaron, recalling his youthful sexual escapades grinned and said, "Yeah, I can remember some good times myself. So, was there anyone particular, any regulars who dropped by to visit her?"

"Yeah, she had many regulars. She had one old man, musta been close to 90, who came by once a week to just lay in bed with her. His wife had been dead for 20 years, and Clarisse never charged him. She just said that he needed to feel the closeness of another human being again. She was like that you know. She cared about people, even when she was charging for sex, she tried to look inside people and see the goodness in them. She was just a kind woman – so kind."

Aaron was beginning to get a clearer understanding of Clarisse, and it appeared that, as was usual, society was too busy condemning to see the good in a person. It is easier to condemn than to look beneath the surface and explore the reasons people are the way they are. Understanding, love, compassion were supposed to be the root of religion, but religion was more about condemnation than love in a world where even the church was nothing but another corporation seeking to maximize profits. Aaron, a look of determination on his face, said, "I'm going to find her killer ma'am. I promise. Any chance you could recall the names of some of her Johns?"

THE GIRL WHO SAID GOODBYE
FOR THE LAST TIME

Motioning for Aaron to follow her into her apartment, she nodded affirmatively. Like all those in a country where the marginal must endure rather than prosper, the apartment was a testament to a society where all the good things flow to those at the top who revel in splendorous luxury while those at the bottom of the economic ladder are nothing more than modern equivalents of serfs from the Middle Ages. Little has changed over the years, as the modern day lords of the manner are no longer called Lords, but rather CEO's and presidents. The modern corporation is now lord of all that lies before it, and people are nothing but commodities to be bought and sold in service to the corporation. Even the consumer has no power over the corporation, because livelihoods and sustenance all come from monolithic entities that are in complete control of the entire world.

The old woman lived in what would be called squalor by polite society. Yes, she was poor, because she chose to be poor according to the propaganda that was spewed out by the government. After all, in America, anybody could make it if they worked hard and struggled. Yeah, tell those born in the ghetto that hard work pays off while the sons and daughters of the elite have the red carpet of opportunity spread out before them. Hard work was reserved for those unlucky enough not to be born into the lap of luxury. How much hard work did the Bushes, the Rockefellers, the Trumps, the scions of wealthy families ever do? After they graduated from Yale or Harvard, where they were admitted because of family connections rather than academic merit, they all became corporate vice-presidents who propped their feet up on a burled walnut desks and started careers at the top rather than the bottom like most people.

The old lady pulled out a chair and motioned for Aaron to have a seat at the kitchen table. She poured him a cup of coffee, and as Aaron watched an army of roaches on the march in a nearby corner, he reluctantly took a sip from what appeared to be an unwashed cup. He would not degrade her by refusing her hospitality, even if it meant drinking from a dirty cup.

She reached up into the cupboard and brought out a spiral notebook. The kind kids used to use when Aaron was in school. She tossed it in front of him and said, "Offered it to the police, but they weren't interested. Just said that there was no need to contact any of her Johns. According to Detective Brennan, the murder was just a random act of violence against a known prostitute who was simply in the wrong place at the wrong time. He did open it and glance through it. He ripped out the second page, put it in his pocket and flipped through the rest and just left it laying there on the table, got up and walked out."

THE GIRL WHO SAID GOODBYE
FOR THE LAST TIME

"John Brennan," Aaron said a disrespectful tone. "I know him well. A real macho guy who loves beating up on suspects. You are poor, then you are guilty. If you are rich, he will figure out a way to ingratiate himself to you. Plays all the angles for his own benefit. His idea of justice is lock-up the poor and throw away the key. The rich, on the other hand, must be treated with respect and catered to, because they are special." Then, as he flipped through the notebook he continued, "Any idea what was on that page he tore out?"

Smiling, the old lady said, "Of course. When Clarisse gave me the notebook, she said, 'Don't read the names in it Minnie.' Now, I like Clarisse a lot, but I am a curious old woman. The name on the page was Warren Cardigan. That isn't a name you would forget in this town. Had his name, number and Park Avenue address."

Aaron sat up a bit straighter and said, "So, you know the Cardigan name. Good for you. He visit her a lot?"

"Well, I can't say. I didn't watch the comings and goings over there that much, but I know she said that there was an uptown guy was crazy about her and was promising to even marry her one day. Said the man was absolutely crazy about her. She couldn't understand why, but he professed to loving her. My guess is it was Cardigan."

THE GIRL WHO SAID GOODBYE
FOR THE LAST TIME

"Well, Park Avenue is certainly uptown, and you can't get much more Uptown Manhattan than the Cardigan family. New York City real estate and that name are almost synonymous. You know Minnie, there is nothing I love anymore than bringing down the high and mighty. It is my favourite past time."

Minnie, laughing out load, said "Go get 'um Mister. By the way, what's your name?"

For the first time in two years, he took a deep breath and said with pride, "I'm Aaron Adams."

"Goddamn. I heard you was dead. You the guy who always sticks up for the poor, always goes after crooked cops and politicians. Can't believe you are still alive and kicking. You gonna get Clarisse's killer, uh?"

Feeling a surge of pride that she recognized his name, Aaron said, "You damn right, or die trying." Then he picked up the notebook and continued. "OK if I take this Minnie? It would be a big help."

"You bet, Mr. Adams. It is yours. Clarisse was a fine woman and she deserves justice. You are the man who can get it for her. I got confidence in you. Ain't many like you left around this here town. Go kick some rich ass!"

THE GIRL WHO SAID GOODBYE
FOR THE LAST TIME

Aaron smiled, turned and walked out of the apartment. He still had to fight depression, but now he had another reason to battle it. He was going in pursuit of justice.

Before seeing Warren Cardigan, Aaron wanted to get a feel for the real Clarisse Coleman. He would talk to a few of her Johns and see what they had to say about here. He wanted to get inside this woman, explore her inner most thoughts and try to understand what made her tick. Only then could he know the real Clarisse and the real reason she was killed.

Page one was a man called Allen Alverson. No address, no phone number, just a name. Well, what would any good detective do? Sure thought Aaron, as he headed toward one of the last phone booths in Manhattan. Hey, everyone, even the poor, was expected to have a cell-phone. Just another grab by corporate entities that were all committed not to serving the consumers, but making the consumers serve them. Try calling to complain and you are expected to go through a retinue of button pushing before they will direct you to the right party, and then you have to wait 30 minutes for some one dollar an hour Third World slave to take your call. Meanwhile, the million dollar a year executives are busy playing golf or enjoying vacations on their yachts. Yeah, welcome to capitalism . What a great system, great for those at the top that is.

There it was, Allen Alverson. Aaron preferred talking in person, as there was so much you could glean from someone by just watching their mannerisms, there tonal inflection, the movement of the eyes or the hesitation in responses. 99465 Lorton Place in Soho.

Aaron had no money for a cab, so he just started walking. It was about 5 kilometres, but what did he have but time. Maybe no energy, but time was a commodity that greeted him each day with no hope. Yeah, he had time to just let his life ebb away. Well, now he had a purpose. He had a case, even if he wasn't getting paid.

Alverson lived on the second floor, and seemed none to happy to see the dishevelled Aaron. "Yes, what can I do for you?"

Aaron loved to watch men squirm. "Clarisse Coleman? Know her?"

Looking back over his shoulder, Alverson, stepped into the hallway and closed the door behind him. He whispered, "What is this about? She's been dead for two years. Keep your voice down. My wife is in the kitchen, and believe me, that old battleaxe is just looking for an excuse to leave me and take everything I got."

THE GIRL WHO SAID GOODBYE
FOR THE LAST TIME

Aaron, aware that not all men who frequented prostitutes were low life scum, decided to give him the benefit of the doubt and whispered, "So, how long did you know Clarisse?"

With a tinge of sincerity in his voice, Alverson replied "About three years. Saw her every two weeks regular. What a woman and I don't mean just sex either. She was a kind soul with a heart of gold. She cared about you. You could just tell. She listened to all my problems and her concern was genuine. You could see it in her eyes."

"So, did she ever mention that she was having trouble with any of her clients? Anything at all that might raise a red flag?"

Shaking his head, Alverson replied, "No, not that I can recall. We did actually talk more than have sex. I went to her for psychological reasons as well as the physical. You know, she was a really smart woman, and she understood that some men like me just want a kind word, someone who seems to care. Wait, wait a minute. There was one time, one time when she said just out of the clear blue that she was concerned about a man who appeared to be in love with her, but that his family would never allow him to marry someone like her. She said that she really cared for him, and she felt he cared for her, but it was hopeless. I just passed it off with little thought, but who knows?"

THE GIRL WHO SAID GOODBYE
FOR THE LAST TIME

"Yeah, who knows? She did not mention a name?"

Aaron, deep down inside, feeling that old antipathy toward the rich and privileged, wanted the killer to be William Cardigan. He needed to one last time bring down the mighty who always thought they were above the law. Yes, that was what Aaron Adams lived for – to bring down those arrogant asses who felt prestige, influence and wealth set them above all others and somehow made them special. Special hell thought Aaron. The real special people were those who toiled in obscurity so those at the top could live their lives of splendorous luxury. With hope Aaron blurted out, "Warren Cardigan? Could that have been the name of the man?"

Instantly recognizing the name, Alverson replied, "No, don't recall her ever mentioning him, but I know the name. That family owns about half of the real estate in the city. You think he was connected to her murder?"

Aaron, choosing his words carefully, said, "Well, I can only wish. I love bringing down the high and mighty. It is what I live for. It is what I have devoted my life to doing, making the exalted actually suffer just a bit like the rest of us do. Making them stand before the bar of justice and tremble with fear for a change."

THE GIRL WHO SAID GOODBYE
FOR THE LAST TIME

A light seemed to go on in Alverson's head. "Yeah, I knew I recognized you. The old clothes, the unshaven face threw me. I know you. You're Aaron Adams. I heard you were dead."

Aaron, flattered that people still recalled him, said, "Not dead, just hibernating for awhile. Thanks, and don't worry about the wife. I'll keep your name out of it."

"You are a righteous dude man. Everyone knows that. Thanks. Let me know if I can help you in any way."

Aaron nodded affirmatively, turned and walked away firm in the knowledge that his life had been worth something. People remembered him as a champion of justice, a man who always stood up for the little guy. Clarisse Coleman was one of the little guys, and he was going to stand up for her, stand up for justice that had been denied because she was not important enough for people like Detective Brennan to pursue her case. Yeah, what had Minnie said? She was a throwaway. Well, not in Aaron's book. She was somebody important, someone who had brought a few minutes of joy to men like Alverson. OK, so she charged a little bit for her company. Go to a doctor, go to a beauty salon, go to a bar, everybody charged. Everything in a capitalist society has a price tag. Clarisse was nothing more than a capitalist.

THE GIRL WHO SAID GOODBYE
FOR THE LAST TIME

CHAPTER 8
HIDE BEHIND A CLOAK OF DECEIT

It is not sexual prostitution that is the obscenity.
It is the selling of one's soul for wealth.
It is the aggrandizement of greed.
It is worship of excess as if it were good.
The poor are reviled for their condition
As if they chose it of their own free will.
The real prostitutes in American society
Are those who put a price tag on human dignity.

Aaron flipped to the next page and there was a name he recognized, Phillip Ambrose. Yeah, he was a stock broker who actually thought stealing millions from people was good business. The suckers were the chumps who stole small change. They got twenty years for robbing a 7-11, while the financiers of Wall Street got a fine and just kept laughing all the way to the bank. People like Ambrose were capitalists of the first order who ruled the system of organized stealing that was sanctioned by a government that catered to those at the top, while throwing a bone to those at the bottom to keep them at bay.

It had been awhile since Aaron had been on Wall Street. He knew where Ambrose's office was, but it wouldn't be easy getting into to see him, especially the way he looked, but Aaron had an ace-in-the-hole, and he was looking forward to playing it. That long dormant arrogance of purpose was working itself slowly back into his psyche. Yeah, he was getting that old swagger back. He felt it as he sashayed down the street with a confident stride, a look of assurance on his face. Damn, he loved taking on the high and mighty!

The secretary was typical Wall Street front office fluff – all looks and no substance. She glared at Aaron like he was some ancient plague come to spread disease on the lords of the manor. He smiled and gave her a wink as he said, "Tell Ambrose that an old friend of his wishes an audience with the potentate of financial manipulation.

With obvious disgust, she replied, "I am sure Mr. Ambrose has nothing he would want to discuss with you."

OK, Aaron could be overbearing at times, but there were times when it was called for, times when arrogance had to be used against those who felt the economic bottom dwellers were pariahs of disgust. This was one of those times.

"Listen you bitch to the baron of greed. Get off your hot little ass, wiggle it into Ambrose's office and tell that high toned robber baron that Aaron Adams wants to see him about Clarisse Coleman."

THE GIRL WHO SAID GOODBYE
FOR THE LAST TIME

The name was enough to send shivers through the woman. "I thought you were dead Mr. Adams."

"Dead or alive, I am here and I want to see Ambrose. Tell him the ghost of Aaron Adams is here if you want, but tell him that he better see me damn quick, or I am handing a little notebook with his name in it to the DA. Move it."

And move it she did. Within a blink of the eye she was back. "Go right in Mr. Adams," she said as she pointed to the door.

Ambrose sat behind a desk that probably came in at around $20,000. He surveyed Aaron up and down, looking appalled at his appearance. "Well, Aaron, I heard you were dead. Looks like they may have been right. You look like you just crawled out of the grave." With a smirk on his face, he continued. "Can I get you anything? A drink, a suit of clothes, maybe a bath?"

Aaron gave him an even more intense smirk. "You can get me some information," Aaron said as he eased into a leather chair that squeaked a bit as he sat down.

"I am a fountain of knowledge when it comes to finances, but I am not certain that is what you are here for, so I am not sure how I can help?"

THE GIRL WHO SAID GOODBYE
FOR THE LAST TIME

"You know what this is about. You like to slum it on occasion, grab a piece of what you consider trash ass. That is why your name was in Clarisse Coleman's little notebook. I am sure a blue-blood high class Park Avenue asshole like you wouldn't want it leaking out that you liked a little slum pussy on occasion. Might not set well with your upper crust friends who do the same thing, but are better at hiding it."

You could see the seething hatred in Ambrose's eyes. "OK Adams. Just because you were smart enough to catch me with my hand in the cookie jar once, which by the way, led to a million dollar fine while I made 4 million on the deal, doesn't give you the right to act all high and mighty around me. Moral do-gooders like you are just whistling in the wind. Nobody is going to stop guys like me from making a buck by playing on people's greed. State your business and take a hike."

Aaron leaned forward a bit and his eyes were daggers. Ambrose could feel the hatred. "So, how often did you see Clarisse?"

His chest puffed out and an arrogant countenance indicated a man who was supremely confident in his superiority. "Whenever I wanted to play my game of sadistic pleasure. I liked to have her lie down and let me piss on her."

THE GIRL WHO SAID GOODBYE
FOR THE LAST TIME

Aaron's disgust was growing. "And how often was that asshole?"

There was that smirk again. "About once a week. Felt real good letting a stream of piss cover her gorgeous body. Made me feel so damn superior." He was almost laughing now.

Aaron rose from the chair. "So, I don't suppose that arrogance got out of control and you decided to see how thrilling it was to actually kill someone up close and personal rather than by stealing their life savings and watch them slowly kill themselves with misery over your thievery."

He actually was laughing now. "Nope, got too much pleasure out of demeaning the bitch. Why take away all that fun by killing her?"

Instincts die hard and Aaron was famous for indignation over arrogance. The old, frail man moved toward the $20,000 desk, reached over and grabbed Amrbose's $500 necktie and pulled him across the desk. Ambrose could not believe the strength the old man possessed.

He pulled him onto the floor and placed his foot right on his chest. "Move asshole and I will crush the life out of you and keep a lot of poor suckers from being taken advantage of. I may be old, but I am not too old to crush arrogance."

THE GIRL WHO SAID GOODBYE
FOR THE LAST TIME

Ambrose couldn't believe he was getting bested physically by an 82 year old man. All he could do was keep as still as possible, because one step and his chest was crushed and his life of greed would slowly ebb away. He was almost whimpering.

Aaron reached down and unzipped his pants. He had that old smile creep across his face, the one that struck fear into the hearts of so many over the years. He pulled out what used to be referred to by women as his instrument of joy, looked down at Ambrose and let lose with a steady stream of piss, smiling all the time.

He shook it off right over his face and said, "That is for Clarisse Coleman and all the others you have pissed on one way or another over the years, and that may not be the end of it. I may come back and take a shit on you if I find out you are the one who killed her Ambrose. I may be old, but I will never be too old to take a dump on assholes like you. When I get too old to kick your ass with my feet, when I get too old to slap your ass with my fists, when I get too toothless to utter a word of contempt I will crawl up on all fours and spit in your face asshole and take my last breath hating you greedy bastards."

He looked down at him and spat in his face, turned and walked out the door. You could hear Ambrose whimpering in the background

THE GIRL WHO SAID GOODBYE
FOR THE LAST TIME

Aaron looked at the secretary and said, "Your boss needs cleaning up. Looks like he finally pissed off the wrong person – and I mean that literally."

It felt good to be alive again, but those feelings of misery simply could not be held in abeyance. Visions of Jasmine played an intense melancholy symphony in his head. The streets were noisy as always with the cars humming along playing the music of hustle and bustle in a city where hope had long ago been tossed to the curb of lost dreams. He looked upward at the towering skyscrapers that were themselves monuments to greed that twinkled against the azure blue sky seeming to move ever skyward in pursuit of that which was inherently unattainable. There was no happiness in greed, only temporary respite from the loneliness of despair. The good life was ballyhooed as easily attainable for those willing to work hard, but truth was much more sobering. That so-called American dream had simply been hijacked by the affluent and powerful who made it a point to keep the good things for themselves and their offspring.

The gold-spangled good life, seeming as if it had been polished by the sun, could be seen at the end of each person's dreams, bristling with hope and, of course, gold. The implacable blue of the sky shone brilliantly overhead as Aaron wandered through the long, cool and sombre corridors of emptiness of the deserted soul of a city where dreams were supposed to be fulfilled, but more often died in the loneliness of despair.

He had wandered into lower Manhattan where the uptown dreams faded into the oblivion of misery and hopelessness. He was alone in his soul, subjected to the stares of prostitutes leaning against doorways or in the alleys, whose eyes seemed to plead for understanding from a society that simply had no heart, no soul, no compassion. Their breasts were brazenly displayed with low cleavage and their arms were bare, their eyebrows were darkened. They wore their hair enticingly long but the stares were blank as you knew they were not living, only existing.

Aaron had been wandering for what seemed like hours and the darkness began to claim the city, wrap it in the blackness that devoured all. He looked at those people who lined the streets, and especially the prostitutes who all seemed to be the living dead. They were just more victims of the plague called greed.

These women stood in solitude among the masses. Surrounded by humanity, but never getting a show of humanity. Their entrails were liquefied by the cold of a society with no soul. Aaron was drawn closer to a motionless girl who was standing by the lamppost where he had met the mysterious lady in the veil. He approached her and she smiled.

"Looking for a good time old man? I can give you good deal tonight. How about 50?"

Aaron smiled and said, "Lady, if I had 50, I would love to just look at you naked. You are beautiful, but I have no money."

Grinning, she relied, "Welcome to the club. Most of the world has no money. It all winds up in the pockets of the few while most of us fight over the crumbs they throw us. Ain't it a shame?"

Aaron instantly liked her. "You a prostitute or a philosopher?"

Laughing, she said, "A little of both, I suppose."

"Well, I prefer the philosopher. You want to humour an old man?"

Nodding her head, she said, "Sure, as long as it doesn't cost me anything."

"No cost, just wondering if you knew a lady by the name of Clarisse Coleman."

"I did, yes. She is dead."

THE GIRL WHO SAID GOODBYE
FOR THE LAST TIME

"I know. You see I am a private detective. I am looking into her death."

A look of concern on her face, the lady said, "That was one nice woman. She once staked me to a meal when I was hard up. She would even pass up a customer if she thought one of the other girls needed the money more than she did. "

"So, you ever meet any of her Johns?"

"No, but she had a steady for about two months before she died. She was off the streets. Rumour was that she was going to marry the guy."

Aaron liked the woman. She exuded a certain kindness, a feeling that you were in the presence of a genuinely caring person who had a soft, tender heart. "You ever hear the name Warren Cardigan?"

"I know the name. Well, the Cardigan name anyway, but never heard it mentioned in reference to Clarisse. I did see her once with a real good looking guy." She pointed to a nearby corner and continued, "Right over there. Saw her get in a chauffeur driven Mercedes. Just caught a glimpse of the fellow inside who opened the door for her. White haired gentleman, maybe early 60's. You know you can tell people with class. He had it and knew it."

THE GIRL WHO SAID GOODBYE
FOR THE LAST TIME

Aaron smiled and said, "Class is a relative thing. For example, I can tell you are a classy lady – a woman with depth of character. Most people being chauffeured in a Mercedes have no idea what real class is. They live life in the backseat of reality. They think money and prestige make you important. What makes a person important is depth of character, the kindness of heart that beats a rhythm of empathy for the downtrodden and the intensity of your compassion. The rich can give millions to charities and pat themselves on their backs, but they are only giving money, not themselves. My dear, I know what designates substance of character and no substance at all."

The woman, beaming with pride that someone had recognized the goodness in her, said, "You are a strange man. What's your name?"

"Adams, Aaron Adams."

There was that old refrain again. "I thought you were dead."

"Believe me; rumours of my death are greatly exaggerated. I may appear to be the walking dead, but I am still very much alive."

Smiling, she said, "I am Lina Olman. You are well known around here. You the man who stands up to the high and mighty."

THE GIRL WHO SAID GOODBYE
FOR THE LAST TIME

Aaron, realizing that all his pride was not gone, felt a surge of self-respect within. "Thank you Lina. I have always tried to do the right thing. I have often faltered, but I have never bowed in supplication to those who think their affluence and power make them somehow a bit better than the rest of us. Bringing down the high and mighty has been my life's work. That life is ebbing away now, but I may have one last chance to right a wrong and make justice prevail."

Lina, a serious tone to her voice, said "Clarisse? You are going to find out who killed her and make them pay."

"You got that right Lina. Whatever it takes I will make sure whoever killed her is brought to justice. No matter how unimportant she may have seemed to the authorities, to me and those who knew her, she was important. To me, she was a woman of character, something that is sorely lacking in a world where most people are concerned with what they can get for themselves rather than what they can do to lift up their fellow man. I am getting to know Clarisse better all the time, and I like her more each day. I wish I had known her personally."

Lina reached out and took Aaron's hand. "Come with me. I have an apartment near here. I'll fix you a hot meal and share my bed with you."

THE GIRL WHO SAID GOODBYE
FOR THE LAST TIME

Aaron, almost in tears, said "are you sure?"

Smiling, Lina said, "Hey, we all need a friend from time-to-time, not someone for sex, but someone who will share the warmth of soul that lifts our spirits. I can tell you are in need of that Aaron."

Aaron was, indeed, in need of the warmth of soul that Lina offered. She was what most would call a low-life, useless, street-walking hussy, but Aaron saw an angel of light who was shining a beacon of kindness that would finally, after two years, wrap him in the arms of hope. Was he going to find his way out of the pit of despair to which he had descended?

There are those who would find a woman of 30 cuddling up in bed with an 82 year old man a disgusting display of affection, but judging affection is like judging character. You never know the depths of one's character until something traumatic occurs and then you can see where a person's true worth lies. Lina was a woman who could see Aaron needed a friend, needed to feel compassion and needed the physical warmth of another person. She saw him not as an old, worn-out man who had lost hope, but as a fellow sojourner on the road of despair that we must almost all travel at times. She saw the good in him, and wanted to let him know that he was still valued and appreciated. Her kind heart was playing a symphony of compassion that wrapped Aaron in her arms and let him regain some self-respect.

As she pointed toward the bathroom, Aaron knew that she wanted him to bathe before lying beside her. He wandered into the bathroom and just soaked in the tub for awhile. A gentle knock on the door was followed by a soft voice that said, "You OK in there Aaron? I have some coffee and a sandwich waiting for you."

"Sure, getting out of the tub right now. Be right there."

OK, Aaron was 82, and as he stood there with a towel wrapped around him, he was no Adonis. He was wrinkled, and his once taunt body sagged and his breasts were the size of a pubescent girl. Yet, there was an intense dignity about him, a certain saviour faire that age could not diminish. Lina smiled and said, "I washed your clothes. They are in the dryer." She pointed toward the kitchen table and continued, "Just use the towel. Your clothes should be dry in about fifteen minutes. I took the envelope out," she said, as she pointed to it laying on the kitchen counter.

Aaron took a seat and stared down at the coffee and sandwich like it was a bountiful feast. He was incredibly hungry and Lina seemed to take great delight in watching him devour the sandwich. She offered to fix him another one, which Aaron gratefully accepted.

As they sat there, Lina stared into his eyes, not with pity but with respect. "I always heard stories about you Aaron. I never dreamed that one day I would be sitting here in my kitchen with you." She got up, moved toward him very slowly and placed her hand on his left shoulder. "I bet you have had a lot of women over the years. A man in your line of work must get a lot of offers."

Aaron, like all men, was proud of that long ago virility that had captivated so many of the ladies. He said with pride, "Well, I did alright in my day I suppose, but that day is long gone."

Lina, sensing that Aaron was in need of an ego boost, said, "Well, you are still an attractive man and a very handsome one too, as age does not diminish looks. It just redefines what good looks are. You, Aaron Adams, are a very sexy older man."

She reached down, took his hand and pulled him up. She moved very slowly toward the bed that was in the far corner of the living room. As she did, Aaron could not believe it, but he felt a rise between his legs. Yes, he was getting an erection.

THE GIRL WHO SAID GOODBYE
FOR THE LAST TIME

Lina stopped at the right side of the bed and said, "You don't mind do you? I find you very appealing."

Aaron, feeling that old mastery of carnality sweep over him said, "Lina, you are a sweet woman who wants to humour an old man, but I am not stupid enough to say no." He swept her into his arms and they passionately kissed, their tongues fighting a duel of passion as they both were overwhelmed with desire. There was no age difference. There was only mutual need and mutual attraction, as time and space seemed to freeze while the two lovers melted into one another's arms.

Lina quickly removed her dress, pulling it up over her head and tossing it on the floor. She had nothing on underneath, and Aaron was aghast at the beauty that stood before him. She cupped her breasts and said, "Suck them Aaron, suck them and savour my tasty nipples that long for your tender suckling." She eased down onto the bed, pulling him with her. She sat on the side of the bed, and continued her pleading, "Suckle like a newborn child my dear. Suck baby, suck and nibble on these big globes of desire and float into the blissfulness of being with a woman who craves to be pounded by that giant tool between your legs." She reached down and pulled the towel away and marvelled at his stiffness and his size.

THE GIRL WHO SAID GOODBYE
FOR THE LAST TIME

As he made chirping noises while devouring first one and then the other breast, she reached down and began to stroke his manhood. Oh, how good it felt. Aaron was a man again. Yes, he felt like a man!

She very slowly manoeuvred him onto the bed, making him lie flat as she worked her way between his legs. At first she blew on his manhood, then she gently kissed it and then, starting at his huge tentacles that were pulsating with delight, she slowly licked her way up the shaft to the tip and at the little slit she teasingly licked the pre-cum up and savoured it like it was the ambrosia of life itself. Then, she very swiftly devoured that instrument of pleasure, swallowing it adeptly until it hit the back of her throat while she began to work it back and forth furiously as if it held within that which was a primal force that would resurrect the dead, light the darkness, quiet the storms of turbulence and calm the mighty seas of despair. She needed for him to explode in her. She had to taste his essence. Within him was the nectar of the Gods. If she swallowed it, she would be a God too. She would be fertilized with the ambrosia of the life force that opened the gates to heaven where all things were possible. She had to have it. Without it, she could not exist. And all the while, Aaron was floating in a sea of blissful contentment as he felt his life force surging upward to release its power.

THE GIRL WHO SAID GOODBYE
FOR THE LAST TIME

Suddenly, he could hold back no longer. Like a volcano blowing its top, he exploded with a fury that nearly blew a hole in the back of Lina's throat so forceful was the explosion of passion. It gushed forth like a raging river flowing over rapids. Oh, how exhilarated they both felt as they collapsed with exhaustion.

Still, the passion would not subside. Aaron reached down between her legs and felt her moisture. She was a wet as Niagara Falls after the spring thaw upstream. Aaron could not understand how she could be so attracted to such an old man, but who was he to ask questions at that point. He massaged her mound of desire and gradually worked his way downward until it was staring him in the face in all its glory, and how glorious it was. Unlike most modern women, Lina had not fallen prey to the manipulation of adult magazines and the razor companies that promoted clean shaven pubes. This was a real woman whose hairy mound was filled with wet beaded residue from her moist womanhood. He nestled in it for awhile, enjoying the aroma of a real woman. He blew on it and then began to flick his tongue out into the moist opening and she sighed with delight. He licked, sucked and blew on it and she began to thrust upwards. She moaned and suddenly a wild spasm seemed to totally engulf her as she let out a long, mournful moan of complete, total satisfaction that brought Aaron as much pleasure as it did her.

J. Wayne Frye

THE GIRL WHO SAID GOODBYE
FOR THE LAST TIME

She reached down and pulled him upwards on top of her. Their mouths met in a passionate kiss as Aaron's stiff member found its way into her opening and he began to rhythmically pound her up, down, back and forth. She was meeting each stroke with an upward thrust and moaning with delight. This was no act thought Aaron. No one could be that good an actress. Lina was actually enjoying sex with an older man.

As the night ebbed away, the two lovers, spent and exhausted, slept contently in each others arms. Aaron had a modicum of contentment back in his life. He had not found love again, but he had found solace in the arms of a genuinely kind woman. He thought to himself that even in death Clarisse was still doing kind things. Had she not been killed, Aaron would not have found contentment and rejuvenation in the arms of Lina.

The next morning brought a round of sex that made both of them look forward to the day. Aaron remembered something his uncle once told him, "Morning sex can make the difference between a good day and a great day." Well, Aaron was about to have a great day.

Lina fixed breakfast and when he left she whispered, "Aaron, my door is always open to you. What happened last night was wonderful. You are the oldest man I have ever slept with, and

THE GIRL WHO SAID GOODBYE
FOR THE LAST TIME

I tell you truthfully, it was the best sex of my life. Please don't be a stranger."

Aaron, feeling some pride and believing that she was indeed earnest, replied. "Lina, I may be 82, but thanks to you, I feel 18."

Lina, smiling, said, "Aaron I am a prostitute and I know most people look with disdain on what I do for a living, but in you, I have found a man who sees the good in me. You do not judge. You look beyond the superficial and see beneath the surface."

Aaron, as he walked out the door, looked back over his left shoulder and said, "The real prostitutes in American society are those who put a price tag on human dignity. You Lina should never hang your head in shame, because you do not hide behind a cloak of deceit."

THE GIRL WHO SAID GOODBYE
FOR THE LAST TIME

CHAPTER 9
THE KILLER OF HOPE

A beautiful sunrise to a dark night
I found you, a kaleidoscope of colour
Longing for love, you reached my core.
Gave me affection I had never felt before.

How I tried to hold onto it;
How I believed in you.
In the dark of night,
From my life faded the light.

Where does love begin and end?
I could not find the source.
Circumstances stood in the way,
Until I could not see the light of day.

Despair covers me in my grave.
Oh, the darkness surrounds me.
Sweet justice must one day reign,
Placing upon my killer the mark of Cain.

Aaron had found new hope in life, but he still had to fight against the despair that kept overwhelming him. Mental illness is a long and difficult battle that afflicts almost all of humanity at one time or another. Most of us are resilient enough to survive its grasp that pulls at our psyches and tries to entrap us permanently in a prison of lost hope. Aaron's battle was not easy at all, as it was, at times, totally consuming and so overwhelmed him that there had been times in his life he had contemplated the ultimate act that frees us from all pain. He carried a gun most of his life, and several times he had taken it in his right hand and placed it to his temple, thinking that was the only way out of the dark pit of despair in which he so often found himself. His life was devoted to helping others, but he could not help himself. As he wandered through the streets of Manhattan, seemingly lost among the throng of humanity that moved about aimlessly in search of that which was unobtainable, he reflected back on that envelope that Jasmine had left. Lina had washed his clothes. Had she opened it? Had she read its contents and knew what Aaron did not know? Oh my, that envelope was his last connection to Jasmine.

He felt his coat pocket, and it was there. He reached inside and pulled it out. Still in tact and not opened. She had no doubt removed it without reading its contents. As he placed it back into his vest pocket, Aaron softly whispered "good woman" to himself. The world was filled with good people, but they did not count in a society where worth was always judged on a balance sheet of dollars and cents. Integrity, kindness, respect for your fellow man had all been sacrificed at the altar of greed in a country that worshipped money, because money was how one's worth was judged. Without money you had no power. Without power you were just another pawn on the chessboard of worthlessness in a corrupt, barren economic system that had devoured and corrupted the world with greed.

Aaron reached into his coat pocket to see if he might have some change to buy a cup of coffee, and inside he felt paper. He pulled the paper out and it was a crisp, new 20 dollar bill. Lina had put it there. Sweet Lina wanted to make sure he had a few dollars to provide sustenance, and people looked upon her as a useless, low-life who was a throwaway in a society that was always pointing a hypocritical finger condemnation. Aaron would take people like Lina over the ministers, the affluent businessmen, the politicians any day of the week. She was the genuine thing, while all the others were just hypocrites who did not know the real meaning of compassion.

Aaron stood in front of a pawn shop and just stared inside. He was stupefied with amazement, dumb, paralyzed. He took a stride towards the door and stopped. He turned his eyes upon a certain spot in the wall, where a little bell was suspended from a leather collar, and underneath it a bundle of string. Yes thought Aaron, in the pawnshop of life, we all hang by a precarious string of ill-contentment with lives that are more struggle than hope. Everyone was trapped in the downward spiral of hopelessness and deep despair but they had all swallowed the propaganda spewed out by the government, corporations and the media that Americans had the best life in the world. The public was simply too stupid and too brainwashed to realize that institutionalized greed, which kept 99% imprisoned to the 1% who ruled supreme, was, in reality, nothing but a prison to keep them in bondage.

Outside an eating-house on Lorton Street, Aaron stopped, and turned over in his mind, calmly and quietly, if he should take a little refreshment. He could hear the rattle of knives and plates inside, and the sound of something being pounded in the kitchen. The temptation was too strong for him. He walked inside.

He took a seat at the counter and said as the waitress waked over, "Beef Manhattan on sour dough please and extra gravy would be nice. I'll have coffee to drink."

"One city hash on sour dough!" shouted the waitress toward the kitchen.

It was somewhat dark in the place as the fluorescent lights were not bright enough, and Aaron felt tolerably well concealed from humanity enough to have a serious think. Every now and then the waitress glanced over at him inquiringly. His first thoughts were of the wonderful night of unbridled sex he had experienced after so many years.

Beginning to wonder if they had to slaughter the cow to get the beef, Aaron glanced toward the waitress and said, "Do you think that beef will be here soon?"

"Coming" she said as she reached back into the counter that opened into the kitchen and lifted up the plate. "Here you are," said the waitress, kindly placing the beef on the counter.

Aaron commenced to eat, and he got greedier as he swallowed whole pieces without chewing them, enjoying himself in an animal-like way at every mouthful, and tore at the meat like a cannibal. He suddenly realized how, with the exception of the prior night with Lina, he had experienced no real "junk" nourishment in two years. Almost laughing, he thought to himself, "Damn, this is almost as good as sex."

The waitress never came over to him again as she had placed the bill down in front of him when she delivered the plate of food.

When finished, he approached the waitress by the cash register and paid the bill, leaving her a one dollar tip, strolled out into the now cloudy dark night and realized where he was.

THE GIRL WHO SAID GOODBYE
FOR THE LAST TIME

There was that infernal lamppost where he had met the veiled woman and Lina. He just stood and stared for awhile, thinking over the events of the past days and wondering if he might just be dreaming. Was he really still in that dingy hotel room lying on the dirty bed staring at the ceiling?

Things became even more dreamlike when total darkness engulfed the entire block, the dark clouds portending a coming storm of monumental proportions. Then, there she was leaning against the lamp-post, the lady in the long black veil again. There could be no mistake about it; she had turned up at the same spot once again. She was standing perfectly motionless. All of a sudden an inspiration seized upon Aaron and he moved swiftly to her.

"Good-evening," said Aaron.

"Hello," she replied.

"I am on the case," chortled Aaron.

"Yes, I know you are. It would not be your style to let a lady down. I appreciate your efforts."

Aaron was wondering if he should ask to see her face, but thought it a bit uncouth, so he did not broach the subject. Rather he just said, "I have talked to Minnie, Alverson and Ambrose."

THE GIRL WHO SAID GOODBYE
FOR THE LAST TIME

"Obviously, thanks to Minnie, you are in possession of that book Clarisse kept with all her tricks listed in it."

"You are right. By the way, what is your name?"

The dark veil concealed her face, but you could sense that behind the veil was a woman of infinite beauty. Still, there was eeriness about the voice, about the looks of the woman behind the veil. The veil was so dark that it hid most vestiges of shape. You could not even see an outline of the face. It was just a voice, but the voice was almost dreamlike, as if it was emanating from beyond the present place and time. She said, "My name is irrelevant. My intent, my purpose is what matters. I intend to let Clarisse rest in peace, because now she is trapped between heaven and hell. She is in limbo until justice is served. You, Mr. Adams, can help me bring her peace."

"I will do all I can," said a contemplative Aaron, "but you have to remember that more times than not, justice is denied, especially to those from the lower rungs of the economic ladder."

You could almost sense a smile behind the veil as she said, "That is why I waited to find you Mr. Adams. You see, I know you are a man who is capable of delivering your own justice if necessary."

THE GIRL WHO SAID GOODBYE
FOR THE LAST TIME

Yes, when true justice was going to be denied, Aaron had done just that. He felt no remorse for the few times he had resorted to being both judge and jury. He recalled the book by Mickey Spillane, *I THE JURY*. In it, Mike Hammer had to resort to being the judge and jury, because there was no other way to bring a killer to justice. Aaron had always been a big fan of Mickey Spillane, even becoming friends with him many years ago when he was in Myrtle Beach, South Carolina on a case. The two had developed an instant simpatico. Yes, there were times when common decency demanded the circumvention of the normal avenues open to rendering justice. In the right circumstances, killing was easy for Aaron.

As he was lost in deep thought, the veiled lady awakened him from his contemplative slumber, "Come with me please."

That seemed a little odd. Aaron stood and pondered over it, and it perplexed him more and more. The street seemed deserted and even the few people strolling by appeared to be animated with disinterest in what was going on between Aaron and the veiled lady. It was as if the two of them stood apart from all else around them, almost as if they were in a dreamlike state. That mist began to rise slowly from the ground and engulf them, seeming to offer cover from the world around them, so they could go about clandestinely in pursuit of the elusive killer of Clarisse Coleman.

They moved on slowly up the street; she walked at his right side. A strange, beautiful feeling empowered Aaron; the certainty of being near a beautiful, mysterious woman was gratifying. He looked at her shapely form the whole way along. The scent of her hair; the sexiness that irradiated from her body; the intoxicating radiance beneath her clothing, the sweet breath every time she turned her face towards him, everything penetrated in an ungovernable way through all Aaron's senses. She had a high bosom that curved out against her cape. The thought of all the hidden beauty which Aaron surmised lay sheltered under the cloak and veil bewildered him, making him titillated. He wanted to touch her with his right hand, but as he reached out to do so, she very sternly said, "No, don't do that please." Then, she stopped and continued. "You see, my body is only reserved for he whom I long for day and night. Are you a man who believes in irrefutable, devoted love of the most intense kind - the kind of love that even goes on after death?

Aaron very sternly replied, "I am, indeed."

She was almost whispering now, "That is how I feel about the man I love. Unfortunately, I am not sure he feels that way about me.

THE GIRL WHO SAID GOODBYE
FOR THE LAST TIME

Aaron sensed she wanted to confide in him, so he said, "I will listen to whatever you have to say."

He could sense she was smiling under the veil as she said, "Sometimes sex is a precursor to all that follows in a pattern called love. I have gone up and down gorgeously arrayed, waiting for he who should loose me from my garments, but he does not come unto me anymore. I long for him to once again wrap me in his arms, but I fear he has forsaken me. Infatuation can be a pattern of deceit as sexuality overwhelms two lovers. I shall tell you of me and my lover. Tell you of how he worshipped a part of my body and devoured me with passion. Do not think me crude. I just want to share with a human being how much this man seemed to adore me."

"He was captivated by what he described as my magnificent ass that lay before him, and he said to me 'How can I help but worship that gorgeous brown pucker-hole. It is so beautiful, and so good to me, because it gives me life. Oh, how I love it. How I savour its smell, its taste, its magnificence, its glory! When my face is between your cheeks, I am in heaven. Yes, I am in heaven, and I don't even believe in heaven.' This was his homage to me which made me feel euphorically delighted that a man could be so overwhelmed with passion for me."

J. Wayne Frye

THE GIRL WHO SAID GOODBYE
FOR THE LAST TIME

"He turned to me in earnest and said, 'I quite adore and love every part of your charming body, but your ass is my home, the place where all my dreams coalesce into a kaleidoscopic prism of eternal light and bliss. I know I am too impetuous and excitable, but I must kiss, fondle, lick, suck and probe the dear source of all my joys.' I know you think me crude by telling you this in such a candid fashion, but I sincerely never had a man so resoundingly infatuated with me like that."

"I could not resist him. Rather I let him savour the delight of my magnificent, glorious hole that attracted him like a moth to a flame. I urged him down between those cheeks, and he applied his lips and tongue to my lovely glorious pucker-hole that was moist with delightful anticipational discharge, which was so sweet to his taste that he first began licking between the folds to sop up all the sweat caused by my cheeks resting together before he got between them, and he meticulously applied himself to my excited, quivering hole, and with his index finger and thumb working furiously, he spread it wide so he could insert his tongue deep within, proving that he was worthy of it. Oh, yes, he had to prove his worthiness, because without that beautiful hole to worship his life would simply ebb away. That hole was his life, yes, without that hole he was destined to fall off the precipice of despair into oblivion and flounder in the corridors of hopelessness. The hole, the hole, the magnificent hole was my sanctifying grace to his desire."

Aaron could not fathom the reason this woman was sharing such intimate details with him, but as they stood in the alleyway, he felt a seminal discharge from the raging erection in his pants. Damn, how he wanted to rip the veil from her and plant a passionate kiss on what was an incredibly alluring woman, slam her against the brick wall behind her and ram his stiff member so far into her mound of desire that the tip of his manhood would tickle her throat.

Without hesitation, she continued. "At night when we were in bed, he slept at the opposite end from me with his face buried between those magnificent cheeks he adored, so anytime in the night he wanted he could lick, kiss and deep tongue it. He said he wanted to make me his queen and make my ass the altar where he worshipped. He told me that I had an ass that should be memorialized for all time. Just to gaze upon it was a privilege and an honour that men would go to war for. Just to gaze upon it was more delight than any man deserved. He said that he would offer sacrifices to it like ancient people who bowed with supplication before idols. He said, "It will be my idol that I shall worship for eternity. Heaven is your smile. Paradise is your giggle. Hope is your sparkling eyes. Salvation is the flick of your hair.

THE GIRL WHO SAID GOODBYE
FOR THE LAST TIME

Your soft melodic voice that whispers like the nightingale is my breath of life and your ass. Oh, your ass is the Rolls Royce of desire. It is the expressway of delight that is my road map of sexual contentment."

She paused for a second, seeming to catch her breath. "Someone who loves life in all its glory and believes that every experience, may it be pleasant or not, is just part of the journey is a person with hope. A person who values trust, loyalty and honesty; someone who is not afraid of risks and challenges is a person who is truly alive. A man who believes that love is not just a programming of one's brain, but a feeling that appreciates, nourishes and guides another individual towards a rewarding and joyous experience is a man with confidence, faith and optimism. I felt this about my lover."

Again she paused and seemed to be in contemplative thought, but quickly continued. "He who cannot see his own flaws of character is a man who will one day pay the price for his wickedness of spirit. The bill for my lover's slights had been unceremoniously rendered from someone else and the price he paid was astronomically beyond that which should be paid by a man who was as poor in spirit as a beggar on a street corner of lost hope. Yet, my lover was paying the price with the agony of loneliness, despair, misery, heartache and woe until I came along. Yes, I was the one who reached out with love, waved my hands and performed the miracle of resurrection. He said that I resurrected him emotionally, but also physically. Yes, between his legs new life sprung ever upward as an erection of desire was once again standing as tall as the Eiffel Tower with his seed willingly gushing forth to deposit its warmth within me. Oh, how I savoured that warmth from him in every cavity of my body."

Aaron's erection was beginning to subside as she continued. "One night I lay beside him, my shapely glorious ass jutting out seemingly begging for his attention. He needed to reach out and touch me. He needed to look into my eyes. He needed to float with bliss hearing me giggle with my soft melodic voice filling the air with the melody of love. He needed my soft, thick lips, my penetrating dark eyes, my mischievous tilt of the head, my coy nature dancing a symphony with bells, symbols and kettle drums in his head constantly. I knew that I was the strings on his violin that played a melody of hope and promise. He was a willing pawn on my chessboard of desire."

She seemed contemplative again. "Good things come to those who are patient and see the silver lining in a dark cloud. That dark cloud may bring rain to water the flower and make it blossom, bringing beauty to the world. So, that which might seem bad at the time, can actually lead to good. My lover had been in the dark, but with me I believed he had been brought into the bright sunshine of utopian, optimistic brightness, because I loved him so deeply."

Aaron was captivatingly overwhelmed by what she had shared with him. He said, "The superficial can lead to the concrete. What might seem superficial can rest on a foundation of concrete and steel that will stand for a thousand years. One is never lost – just not found. You were, no doubt, the searcher who was offering this man the chance to be found. His adoration of your ass was only a manifestation of his true devotion to you as the woman whom he adored. You must find him and embrace him. You must let him know that in your arms he is home."

Again, he sensed she was smiling beneath the veil. "You do not know it Aaron Adams, but you, by solving this case, will also solve my dilemma of love. You will offer me salvation or damnation, depending on what you find. I know you have your own demons that you must fight constantly to keep from falling into the abyss. You, too, shall find what you are looking for. You shall find the peace that seems so elusive right now. Believe me, all is not lost. Together we will walk down the road that will lead us to the answers we seek – the answers that will set us free."

She lifted her right hand and with a waving motion said, "You cannot follow me where I go." Then the mist seemed to move upward toward her waist and creep down the alleyway as if leading her somewhere unknown. She began to almost float as she moved with the mist and turned her head back, looking over her right shoulder to say, "You shall find he who bears the mark of Cain – the mark of the killer of hope."

THE GIRL WHO SAID GOODBYE
FOR THE LAST TIME

CHAPTER 10
WHO PICKED UP CLARISSE

Justice denied the poor is a dark blight
That is rarely rectified by those with might.
Yet, within the hearts of the devout few
Beats the rhythm of retribution tried and true.

As Aaron walked out of the alleyway, to his surprise there was none other than a smiling Lina Olman. "Well, Mr. Aaron Adams. How nice to see you again. Are you ready for another night of bliss?"

Aaron bowed his head sheepishly, "Considering all things, you ought not to walk with me. I disgrace you right under every one's eyes, not with just my age but with my shabby attire."

She looked directly at Aaron. "Indeed. I would think it would make me proud to be seen with such a distinguished older gentleman."

Aaron, shaking his head, said, "Thanks for the 20. Lina you are an exceptional woman who deserves the best. Believe me, I am not it."

Lina, in a stern and direct voice said, "Aaron Adams, I will be the judge of that not you."

Aaron smiled as he said, "Yes ma'am."

THE GIRL WHO SAID GOODBYE
FOR THE LAST TIME

This was another blissful night for the two, as they found solace in each others arms. However, Aaron made it plain to her that she was only a way station on his way to the grave, as he would never get over Jasmine, and that no amount of fornicating would diminish the emptiness he felt without her."

Lina said, "Aaron, why will you not go in supplication to her and beg forgiveness?"

"There is no forgiveness left in her. It has all been used up. It is my destiny to die in loneliness, pinning for her. I am simply a lost soul who cannot be found."

Lina reached out and touched his frail left arm as they sat at her kitchen table. "I found you Aaron. One day she will find you, too. Just wait and see. She will come back to you when she realizes she lost the best part of her. Give her time."

Aaron smiled and said, "Thank you Lina. I love you. I hope you know that."

"Of course I know you love me, Aaron, and I love you. It is much more than sex. We need each other, and we have found a simpatico with each other that gives us comfort. So, tell me, what is on your agenda for today. Is this the day you bring the final curtain down on Clarisse's killer?"

THE GIRL WHO SAID GOODBYE
FOR THE LAST TIME

Aaron, feeling a surge of energy, said, "It may be. You said that you saw her get into a car with a distinguished looking white haired gentleman. That could not have been Warren Cardigan, as he is only 37 years old. I am going to see Warren today. I believe I have a good idea of what happened, but I want to be sure before I make any accusations."

The two shared an embrace and parted. Aaron knew that he had found someone who was more than just a brief respite from his misery. Lina was a friend who was genuine, tried and true. She was that rare commodity in a society where people were taught from an early age that greed was a good and envious trait. A society that utilized brainwashing to make each American feel they were special, because they were part of a culture that was steeped in old-time religion, which meant they were favoured by God as a nation of destiny, and each individual in that nation was somehow better than people in other countries. Lina was the exception; she saw through the façade of manipulative reverence for greed and reached out with compassion to those trapped by that adherence to a bankrupt philosophy of lost hope for all but the few. She was a woman of exceptional quality who stood above the norm and radiated the same kind of light Aaron saw in his dear Jasmine. She was woman of the night who was looked upon with disdain by polite society, an associate of whores, thieves and low-lives who were somehow unworthy of respect. In truth, those who should have had no respect whatsoever were the real thieves, the real whores, the actual low-lives who sat in their splendorous mansions, the opulent board-rooms of corporations, the leather seated back of limousines and stole from widows and orphans, associated with the real low-lives of society – the bankers, the politicians who sold their souls for wealth and power. Those, not Lina, were the real whores of America.

The Cardigan Towers were on Park Avenue near Hunter College. It was twin 88 story skyscrapers that were just another monument to greed in a city where greed was the religion that most people worshipped. Ballyhooed as the realization of a dream for immigrants who arrived on its shores, the city had chewed up more immigrants and made them slaves to the high and mighty than it had ever lifted out of poverty. That was the problem with capitalism. It had a moneyed class that was supposed to be envied, and those at the bottom were taught to aspire to be part of that moneyed class. After all, in America, anybody could make it. How stupid thought Aaron. The very nature of a system based on greed made it mandatory that the few at the top who enjoyed a splendorous existence could only maintain that lifestyle on the backs of those kept at the bottom of the economic ladder. Without the poor, there could be no upper class. The upper class obtained their exalted status on the backs of the poor. That was why immigration was so important to the moneyed class. It kept a steady supply of cheap labour rolling in, which in turn kept the workers eternally afraid of losing jobs and thereby, not demanding too much in wages. The system had always worked well, but in 1980, the Hollywood boob, Ronald Reagan, sanctified greed, destroyed the power of unions and gave the green light to corporate mergers that solidified the complete control of the American economy for the 1%. He drove the final nail in the coffin of hope for the middle class.

Suddenly, Aaron was at the Cardigan Towers and stood in awe contemplating how one man could be allowed to have so much, when so many slept in alleyways, doorways or under cardboard boxes. What kind of evil allowed the few to live lives of excess while most people were on their knees begging for a crumb from the table of plenty? Where were the churches that were supposed to represent the man who admonished the rich to give all they have to the poor? Where were the politicians who promised to support the interests of the middle class and poor? Where were the unions that were supposed to protect the working man? And where were the people who should be storming through the lobbies of the corporations demanding fairness?

THE GIRL WHO SAID GOODBYE
FOR THE LAST TIME

Aaron reflected on that old adage, "people get the government they deserve." Yeah, maybe that was so, but there was never any real choice, because, in America, there were only two parties in control. Democrats and Republicans were different names, but when you peeled off the wrapper, what was underneath was exactly the same. Nobody served the people. They served themselves with lavish salaries, parsimonious benefits and the nearly guaranteed right to keep their jobs for life, and when they did retire, they sat in the boardrooms of the corporations which they really served rather than the people who elected them. Damn, how Aaron detested people like the Cardigans. They represented evil of the foulest kind. Well, he might be a down and out private eye reduced to living on Skid Row, but he was still Aaron Adams, and he still had some fight left in him. He still had the energy to bring down the high and mighty one last time and then crawl away into a dark corner and simply die, longing for she who had deserted him. His life was over, but maybe he could destroy the Cardigans and their arrogance before his final exit. No doubt, Warren Cardigan had just played with Clarisse's affections, believing that he had the right to use and abuse her simply because of who he was. How delightful it would be to bring the high and mighty down one last time. That had been his life, and maybe it could be savoured one more time at his death.

J. Wayne Frye

THE GIRL WHO SAID GOODBYE
FOR THE LAST TIME

Like the rest of America, security was always paramount at the entrance to corporation offices. After all, the paranoia after 9/11 had led to massive security measures and the curtailment of rights, but the sheep of America just accepted the abrogation of their freedoms willingly in order to fight the evil of those who had been propagandized into devils. How stupid thought Aaron. The real devils were America's own government and corporations that kept trying to rule the world and make it a giant playground for the industrial giants that wanted to gobble up every Third World country's resources to fuel their machinery of exploitation and satisfy the insatiable, avaricious greed for more and more. The American people could not understand the commitment and bravery it took for the perpetrators of 9/11 to die flying those planes into those buildings, nor the reasons they were driven to commit such a dastardly act by a nation that wanted to rule the entire world with its commitment to greed. Nor could they understand the cowardly, ineffective response from that buffoon of banality, George Bush, who thought it brave to hurl missiles from 4000 kilometres away and rain bombs down from 80,000 feet on a backward nation of people who were just as much in bondage to religion as the American people were in bondage to corporate greed. In reality, the average American actually had a great deal in common with those terrorists who flew the planes into the buildings. They were all repressed by powerful interests that were imprisoning them in hopelessness. The average American had nothing in common with President George Bush, who sat out the Vietnam War because of his privileged status and had spent his life being bailed out of failed businesses by his father and his rich Arab friends. The commonality was between the average American and the so-called terrorists, as they all had been kept down by moneyed interests. Yet, the gullible American public genuinely believed using terrorism to fight terrorism was justified. They could not see that they were the victims of government and corporate terrorism every day of their lives and that the attack on the twin towers was an attack on greed and all it represented in a world that served the interests of the 1% while ignoring the 99%. "Damn," whispered Aaron under his breath. "I am getting that old feeling of indignation and wrath back again. Only if I still had Jasmine by my side, yeah, I might go out a fighting old man, railing against the evils of capitalism."

As he walked through the metal detectors toward the armed guards, he thought how ironic that people thought this was freedom, having to live in fear. How stupid. By causing all this paranoia about security, the terrorists and the now dead Osama Bin Laden had already won the war and the American public was too stupid to see it.

THE GIRL WHO SAID GOODBYE
FOR THE LAST TIME

One of the guards looked intently at Aaron. Maybe he recognized him, thought Aaron. Aaron moved toward the huge, circular reception desk and a Barbie Doll that had, no doubt, spent hours under the surgeon's scalpel to attain what she thought was perfection, through collagen injected puffy lips said, "Yes, may I help you sir?"

Aaron wanted to blurt out, "No, but I can help you by telling you that no matter what you looked like before, it had to be better than this plastic façade that makes you look ridiculous as a woman of 40 trying to appear to be 20. Be yourself and be proud of who you are, and stop falling for the marketing hype that controls and manipulates you."

Of course, being more valorous than that, all Aaron said was, "Warren Cardigan, please."

Very sternly, she replied "I am sorry, but you must book an appointment to see Mr. Cardigan."

Aaron, feeling that old verve and self-confidence, said "Just tell him Aaron Adams is here to discuss Clarisse Coleman's demise with him. He'll see me."

A look of shock came over her face as she murmured, "Aaron Adams, I thought you were dead."

THE GIRL WHO SAID GOODBYE
FOR THE LAST TIME

Aaron, with a determined grimace replied, "No, I am very much alive, and I want to see Mr. Cardigan, now."

She said, "Sure, sure. I will contact him. Just a second."

Standing there, Aaron was astounded how he was still remembered, even by people who thought him dead. He listened intently as the woman spoke into her headset, "There is a Mr. Aaron Adams who needs to see Mr. Cardigan."

She began steadily nodding her head as she emphatically said, "I know, but he says tell Mr. Cardigan it is about the death of Clarisse Coleman and he will see him. You don't understand," she continued, "this is the famous private detective, Aaron Adams."

It was then that Aaron laughed out loud, as the woman said, "No, he isn't dead. He is standing right here in front of me."

She looked up and smiled at Aaron, as she was obviously waiting for her to inform Warren Cardigan that Aaron wanted to see him.

Forcing a smile on her plastic face, she nodded, pointed to the elevator and said, "Express elevator will take you to the 64th floor. Just step off into the corridor and Ms. Blain will take you right in to Mr. Cardigan's office."

The elevator was obviously a precursor to the opulence of Mr. Cardigan's office. The interior was not metal, but Corinthian leather that wrapped around the walls like a tight fitting glove, making you feel warm and cozy. The music was soft and mellow and even the ride up was so smooth it hardly felt like you were moving. This was no normal Otis elevator. Aaron looked on the door and embossed in gold on the leather was the word Krupp. This was Germany's finest. Yeah, the same company that made billions building arms for Hitler's war machine was now building opulent elevators for the elite of the business world. Well, Hitler's military destroyed everything in its path, and now corporations did the same thing. Krupp must have felt right at home in the corporate world. Corporations and Hitler, two peas in the pod, they both had ambitions to conquer the world. Hitler lost, but the corporations won. The corporations didn't have concentration camps; they had sweat shops all over the Third World. Hitler burned people up in ovens, corporations burned up their souls and then tossed them into the trash heap along with other commodities that had been used up.

The door opened automatically and Aaron stood in awe at the splendour before him. Just one more example of the arrogance of the rich thought Aaron. Moderation could have been used for the executive offices and the money used to benefit the employees who were the real backbone of the company, but no, waste for those at the top was more important than a hand of compassion for those at the bottom. It was the way of a world where the few simply thought all things should flow to the top to serve the needs of those who reaped the real benefits of unbridled capitalism. Fortunes were built on the backs of working men and women, but there was no consideration for them, only those at the top were to be pampered and exalted. The utter disregard for common decency was abundantly clear.

The corruption of power is absolute. As the magnificently attired young receptionist moved toward Aaron, with a, no doubt, focus group practiced smile on her face and an extended hand that sported a manicure that probably cost $200, Aaron was overwhelmed by the opulence of the reception area. The floor was obviously imported Italian marble and the walls were sprinkled with gold that sparkled from the light cast on it by magnificent chandeliers that hung from the 20 feet high ceiling that was also gold inlayed. The place smacked of corporate arrogance that was the norm for a world where greed was brazenly displayed with no consideration for the crassness and utter distaste to flaunt such opulence in a world where one-third of the people were forced to live on less than a dollar. Aaron wanted to whip out his cock and take a piss on the floor just to show his utter disdain for such arrogance, but he managed to restrain himself as the young lady shook his hand and said, "I understand you want to see Mr. Warren Cardigan."

Aaron replied, "I do."

She turned and pointed toward a door to the right that had large gold letters that read, *Warren Cardigan, Vice Chairman of the Board*. To the left was a larger door that read, *William Cardigan, Chairman of the Board*. The lady opened the door and said, "Mr. Adams, sir."

First impressions are sometimes wrong, but rarely. Aaron had already formed an opinion about the Cardigans even before he walked into the building. The opulence that surrounded him didn't diminish Aaron's feelings of disdain. Warren Cardigan's office could have been lifted from Versailles as its opulence far surpassed what he had seen in the reception area. Majestic in appearance yet intimate in scale, the office reflected a garishness that was almost overwhelming. The elegance was mesmerizing to the eyes, and as Warren Cardigan rose up from his high-backed antique chair and moved around to the front of the desk to shake Aaron's hand,

THE GIRL WHO SAID GOODBYE
FOR THE LAST TIME

Aaron was a bit surprised my the meekness that seemed to be a part of Warren's physical makeup. He had no intimidating stride, nor did he bear himself with arrogance which was common among the elite of the corporate world. He was maybe 6 feet tall, but not intimidating at all. There was sadness about his countenance, almost as if he wanted to apologize for his affluence. He was a handsome man in his late 30's, but not handsome to the extent that one would be overly impressed with his looks. It was a quiet, unassuming handsomeness, and one felt that beneath the exterior was a man who was not happy with his lot in life. Aaron wanted to dislike him, but was having a hard time doing it.

As he shook Aaron's hand, he said, "I know. I know it is an ostentatious display of arrogance. Believe me, if I had a say-so, which I don't, I would be in a more modest office." He pointed at a sofa in the corner and walked over with Aaron. They had a seat and he continued, "I had heard you were dead. Obviously an erroneous rumour."

Aaron, smiling, said, "I am pleased to say that, yes, it is just a rumour. Although, of late, the rumours are beginning to make me question whether I am breathing or not."

Laughing out loud, Warren asked if he would like something to drink. Aaron replied, "No."

THE GIRL WHO SAID GOODBYE
FOR THE LAST TIME

Aaron was a man who always tried not to be judgmental, but he had found through experience that the majority of the privileged class was arrogant and self-absorbed. Yet, he found himself immediately liking Warren. For some reason, that bothered him, as he assumed through deductive reasoning prior to meeting him, Warren was, no doubt, the killer of Clarisse. Now, he wasn't so sure.

Aaron decided to cut through the niceties and get to the point. "Warren," (Aaron never showed deference toward those with wealth, power or position by calling them Mr., Ms., or even his or her majesty), "I am here about the death of Clarisse Coleman. Frankly, I believe a lot of circumstantial evidence in regards to her murder points directly at you."

Warren, bowing his head and sighing, said "I can understand that Mr. Adams. I would certainly put myself at the top of the suspect list. I was amazed that Detective Brennan was so cursory in his questioning of me. He was in this office about five minutes, and apparently satisfied that I was innocent. I assume you will be a bit more difficult to convince."

"Well, Detective Brennan is not known as one who is very adapt at doing his job when it involves people with position, power and money."

THE GIRL WHO SAID GOODBYE
FOR THE LAST TIME

Again Warren sighed, "Yes, and I know your reputation. What person of wealth or power in this city doesn't? You are a man with a stellar reputation when it comes to never allowing anyone's position, power or money to hinder you from exacting justice. I admire that about you."

Aaron, proud of his reputation, felt the sincerity in Warren's voice. He was a wealthy man who did not exude the arrogance Aaron expected. In fact, he found himself trying hard not to like Warren. "In all honesty, I have very little respect for those who make their money on the backs of others and do not share the largesse. I would put the Cardigan Empire in the category as one of the most maleficent of the capitalist corporations of greed."

"You are certainly right Mr. Adams. You see, I am a weak man who has never been able to stand up to his father but once in my life. I have lived the life he planned, not the one I wanted. I have been a disappointment to him, because he says I am too kind hearted, too weak to run a successful business."

Aaron, who had heard the same thing from his own father, felt great empathy with Warren. "I can empathize with you Warren. It is often difficult to stand up to a powerful figure like your father, and even more difficult to satisfy his expectations. However, that is no excuse for murder."

THE GIRL WHO SAID GOODBYE
FOR THE LAST TIME

Warren, tears forming in his eyes, said "I did not kill Clarisse. I loved her. In fact, I was prepared to give all this up for her. Two days before her murder I told my father about our relationship, and that I was leaving my wife, who, by the way, he had picked out for me, and moving in with her. I made it clear that none of this meant anything to me without her. I was prepared to take any lowly job and support her Mr. Adams. I would have sacrificed my own life for her. She was the most extraordinary woman I ever knew. Since her death two years ago, I, too, have been dead. I am breathing, but I have no life. All I do is pine for her." Then the tears began to flow in earnest. "I am sorry Mr. Adams, so sorry." He wiped his tears and bowed his head.

Aaron, touched with Warren's display of emotion, said "It is OK. Believe me; I have cried many tears myself the last two years. I don't think you killed her now, but I must find her killer. There is a woman in a long black veil…" It was then that Warren perked up, almost as if he recognized who the woman might be, as Aaron continued, "Who has hired me to do so. I cannot rest until I bring Clarisse's killer to justice. Is there anything you can tell me that would be of assistance?"

Still seemingly in deep thought, Warren responded, "No, nothing that comes to mind."

THE GIRL WHO SAID GOODBYE
FOR THE LAST TIME

"Did you know any of her clients?"

Looking somewhat offended, Warren replied, "No, I insisted she stop seeing other men after our third date. I could not countenance her being with other men. She agreed, as she said that she, too, had fallen in love with me, and I knew it had nothing to do with money, because I never told her who I was. I used an assumed name, because I was ashamed of my real name, ashamed to let her know that she was in love with someone from such a despicable family with a reputation as slum lords. She never knew my last name, only Warren." He then seemed to be contemplative and continued, "Mr. Adams, do you know who the woman in the black veil is?"

"I have never seen her face, only heard her soft melodic voice and sensed the power of kindness and love within her. Do you know who she is?"

Warren, making that customary sigh, said "No, no I can't be sure," but he was sure, Aaron knew.

There are some thing's better left alone, and Aaron decided it was not the time to pursue whether he knew the woman in the veil or not, as it was not crucial to solving the case at that point. He decided to pursue another line of questioning. "Did you ever meet any of her friends while you knew her?"

THE GIRL WHO SAID GOODBYE
FOR THE LAST TIME

"I did meet her neighbour briefly, but she probably just thought I was one of her customers. She also pointed out a woman one night who was by the lamppost where I first met her. Called her Lina and said she was a nice person. That was all I am afraid."

Aaron leaned toward Warren and very confidently said, "I'll find her killer, Warren. I am as tenacious as a Pit Bull with his mouth around a sliver of meat. Detective Brennan is not a man to be trusted. I am always leery when he is on a case. There is a reason why this case was shelved. He is as crooked a cop as you will ever find, and they are all, for the most part, crooked in one way or another. It is the nature of those who wield power to somehow think they are just a bit better than the average Joe. Their job is to keep the rest of us in line for the power brokers like your father. The police, the affluent, the corporate executives and the politicians have a different set of rules than the rest of us. My life has been devoted to bringing down the high and mighty, and I am going to do it one last time. I warn you, if you father is involved, he will be brought down, too."

Warren, without any hesitation, said, "Do what you must Mr. Adams. You have my support. In fact, may I give you a retainer and ask that you work for me as well as the lady in the black veil. I have a suspicion you are doing this job gratis."

THE GIRL WHO SAID GOODBYE
FOR THE LAST TIME

Aaron needed money, and he felt no remorse when he said, "I could use a couple of hundred."

Warren walked over to his desk, opened a drawer and walked back with a wad of $100 bills. He handed them to Aaron. "Whatever is there consider it a retainer. You need any more just let me know. And please keep me posted on things."

It was wonderful to be wrong about a rich person thought Aaron as he got up, firm in the belief that Warren was not his man, and that he was also not the typical man of affluence. It felt good to find a genuine person among the potentates of high finance. He shook hands and walked out of the office. Just as he stepped into the corridor, the door to William Cardigan's office flung open and out walked an immaculately attired distinguished looking white haired gentleman.

Aaron proceeded toward the elevator, but looked out of the corner of his eye as the man talked to the receptionist who had ushered Aaron into Warren's office. The man frantically picked up a phone at the reception desk and had a very animated conversation. The elevator door opened and Aaron walked in, turned and looked back at the white haired man. Their eyes met in an intense stare, and Aaron knew it was William Cardigan, and that he was, no doubt, the man in the chauffeured Mercedes who picked up Clarisse.

THE GIRL WHO SAID GOODBYE
FOR THE LAST TIME

CHAPTER 11
DARKNESS WOULD FALL ON A KILLER

Like a Shakespeare sonnet of old
The truth can forever be told.
Some glory in their birth, some in their skill,
Some in their wealth, some in their body's force,
Some in their garments project affluence;
And every humour hath adjunct pleasure,
Wherein it finds a joy above the rest:
But these particulars are not fine measure,
Love is better than high birth to any with passion.
Richer than wealth, prouder than garments' cost,
Of more delight than treasures be;
Having love, of all men's pride can boast:
Wretched in this alone, that someone can take
All this away, and a life most wretched make.

As Aaron exited the building, he noticed a grey Mercedes parked out front. He kept glancing out of the corner of his eye and it slowly crept through traffic, keeping a distance of maybe 100 metres, but it was obvious that Aaron was being followed. The call made by William Cardigan was obviously to his chauffeur who was now shadowing Aaron. No matter, Aaron had been followed by better. Anyway, if you had a protagonist following you, at least you knew where he was. He gave no thought to nefarious intent at the time, as he just assumed that William Cardigan was curious about what he was up to.

THE GIRL WHO SAID GOODBYE
FOR THE LAST TIME

Shaking the tail was easy for an old pro like Aaron. He walked into the Dunray Building where his office used to be, and a stunned doorman said, "Aaron Adams. I thought you were dead."

Aaron smiled and said, "Maybe I am Frank. Do me a favour. Walk out front, go over to that grey Mercedes and tell the driver, Mr. Adams said fuck you."

Frank nodded, smiled and said, "You bet Aaron."

Meanwhile, Aaron ducked back thought the rear exit, down the alley and over to the adjacent street. He was going to see Minnie, as it occurred to him there was something she might have overlooked about Clarisse – something that was crucial to finding her killer.

Minnie was effervescently delighted to see Aaron and asked him in for a cup of tea, which Aaron, despite his need for haste, thought was a nicety in response to her obvious loneliness that he could not refuse. As they sipped on tea, Aaron said, "Minnie, I have been thinking about what you said in regards to never meeting any of Clarisse's tricks. Are you absolutely sure you never saw anyone around here, perhaps a white haired man, very distinguished looking, about 60 years old?"

THE GIRL WHO SAID GOODBYE
FOR THE LAST TIME

A light seemed to flash on in her head, "Of course, yes I did see a man there about two days before her death. I was coming back from the corner grocery. I never thought he was leaving her apartment; but sure, he must have been, because he wasn't visiting me, and he was coming up the stoop as I rounded the corner. He walked directly to a fancy-looking grey car, got in the back and it drove off. Sorry I forgot about that. Is it significant?"

"It is Minnie, very significant. I think I am beginning to put the pieces of a rather nefarious puzzle together, and a lot of people are going to be very upset when the truth comes out. One other question, had you ever seen Detective Brennan before he questioned you? Think really hard."

"Well," she said as seemingly in deep thought, "maybe, I do recall thinking he looked familiar, but I am not sure. Ummm, let me think a moment."

Then she blurted out, "Of course I had seen him before. He was standing by that grey car that pulled off with the white haired gentleman. He was on the driver's side, talking to the chauffeur when the man got in. Before the white haired guy got in, he said something to Brennan and Brennan nodded his head, walked away from the car as it pulled away and he was staring at Clarisse's apartment. He just stood there for a few seconds staring. Yeah, I remember it all now. I am sorry that I did not remember earlier."

"It's OK Minnie. The mind stores information in its recesses that seem to crop up at the most opportune times. This is one of those times. You have been a big help. I'll let you know how much once I put all the pieces together."

Minnie seemed delighted, and as she escorted Aaron to the door she said, "You are a righteous man Aaron. There ain't many like you around anymore. Most people just wouldn't a cared about Clarisse."

One last question popped into Aaron's mind as he thought to himself that he might not have cared either if it wasn't for the woman in the black veil. It was then that he said, "Minnie, you ever seen a woman in a long black veil around here. She is probably a prostitute, too."

Minnie, her eyes getting glassy looking and enlarged, replied "Of course, Clarisse would often wear a black veil after meeting that man who took her off the streets. She said that she was ashamed for old clients to see her, because she didn't want them bothering her for sex. She hated having to tell them no and explain things. She was proud to be off the streets, but still had feelings for all those who had come to depend on her kindness and compassion as well as for sex. She just wanted to avoid them. Why?"

Aaron, mystified, replied, "Not sure Minnie. I was just curious that's all."

Aaron left, but he could not get what Minnie said out of his mind. As he meandered up the street, he thought he saw that grey Mercedes pull into a nearby alley. No, he thought, couldn't be. I shook that guy back at the Dunray building. Too bad Aaron's mind had began to wander back toward the misery which had trapped him for two years, because he might could have prevented a murder otherwise. The depression and deterioration of his mind had subsided, but it had not been arrested, because a sudden moroseness seemed to overwhelm him as he glanced across the street at a woman who reminded him of Jasmine. Thus began a fog of misery that clouded his mind and made him temporarily forget how important it was to find Clarisse's killer. Little did he know that his decent back into the madness would cause a hellacious series of cataclysmic events that would lead to not just one murder, but two. He was once again on a downward spiral into a dark pit of hopelessness. It was as if a dark hole had opened up, swallowed him and he was free-falling downward, ever downward into a pit of despair that covered him in blackness.

THE GIRL WHO SAID GOODBYE
FOR THE LAST TIME

In his mind, Aaron went over that which had brought him so low:

The first night we met
I knew it to be true
This girl standing before me
Was genuine and true.

I looked into your eyes.
The deep browns didn't lie
You loved me so very much
I knew by your soft sigh.

The nights turned into mornings.
The days went by far too quick.
My sickness let the love slip away,
As it was just impossible to lick.

Then finally the day had come
You said you couldn't wait.
Time had passed so swiftly.
Now, it was far too late.

It was then I realized
I made a huge mistake.
I let the girl I loved
Simply slip away, simply slip away.

The case had kept the demons at bay, but now they were once again at play in a mind that was again deteriorating into despair.

THE GIRL WHO SAID GOODBYE
FOR THE LAST TIME

*When you love someone
who doesn't love you back,
when you've given so much
of your mind, body and soul
and you long for her to care,
the hurt is your greatest fear.*

*When she is all you think about
be it morning, midday or night,
the hurt sears deep within
and scorches your soul.
How you long for that which was,
but now in her has taken pause.*

*When they don't call or e-mail
you spend another lonely night
in the despair of lost hope.
The pain and hurt bypasses your heart
and cuts deep into your soul
where it festers dark like a clump of coal.*

*You think of that other man
who now has captured her heart.
You cannot understand how she
can love someone so dark.
Why doesn't this woman understand
that she has put you in a barren land?*

*When you have cried a river of tears,
given your all and cursed your fate,
when you realize it is just too late,*

J. Wayne Frye   223

THE GIRL WHO SAID GOODBYE
FOR THE LAST TIME

when you have apologized, begged
pleaded and supplicated yourself in despair,
you finally realize that life is not fair.

When you ride that roller coaster of emotion
with all its ups and downs and you
are depressed and angry at yourself
for loving her so much it hurts,
you look back on the mirth you had
and try hard not to be so sad.

Strolling through the streets of agony,
You know what is forever gone.
There is no hope now to recover
That which has been so sorrowfully lost.
Deep within you pray for the end
As no hope can anyone lend.

Aaron I walked on and become more and more sombre; felt languid and weary, and dragged his legs after him. It began to snow. By a Catholic church, he brushed the snow off a bench in front of it and sat down to rest as tears filled his eyes. All the passers-by looked at him with much astonishment as he sat there weeping. But this was New York City, so no one bothered to ask his dilemma or offer a hand up.

Aaron thought to himself, "what a miserable plight I have come to! I am so heartily tired and weary of my miserable life that I do not find it

J. Wayne Frye

worth the trouble of fighting any longer to preserve it."

Adversity had once again gained the upper hand; it had been too strong for Aaron to fight. He had become so strangely poverty-stricken and broken, a mere shadow of what he once had been; his shoulders were sunken right down on one side, and he had contracted a habit of stooping forward fearfully. He had examined his body a few days ago, in his room, and stood and cried over its deterioration.

He sat there in the cold on the bench and pondered his fate, forgetting Clarisse. He began to loathe himself. Even his hands seemed distasteful to him; the loose, almost coarse expression of the backs of them pained him, disgusted him. He saw himself as a loathsome creature. He looked at his gaunt, shrunken body, and shrink from bearing it, from feeling it envelop him. If the whole thing would come to an end now, I would heartily, gladly die he whispered to himself.

Completely worsted, soiled, defiled, and debased in his own estimation, he rose mechanically and commenced to walk into what he felt was oblivion, as he felt completely aimless. On the way to nowhere, he passed a door and at its base was an old man huddled up under newspapers, shivering from the cold.

THE GIRL WHO SAID GOODBYE
FOR THE LAST TIME

While the wealthy and powerful dined on caviar and downed dry martinis, the poor, like the man in front of the door, were forgotten throwaways in a society that had no core. Instead of helping the poor with a dose of Jesus, the churches should have their members marching on the Mall in Washington, DC demanding a fair distribution of income thought Aaron. What would the church's beloved Jesus be doing? Wouldn't he be chasing the money changers from the square? Wouldn't Jesus be down on Wall Street railing against the evils of greed and lashing out at those who robbed and stole their way to the top? Welcome to America – the land of religion and greed. People were more concerned about keeping their rapacious guns than giving a hand up to their fellow citizens. Hey, you needed guns to protect yourself from the poor, who might one day decide they had enough and start marching on the banks and taking the money, going into corporate owned grocery stores and removing food from the shelves without paying. They might finally get some courage and stand up against the greed that had an iron-fisted grip on a country that had sold its soul for a few pieces of silver.

Aaron had never had any use for God, even as a boy. He saw religion as the invention of the wealthy to keep the poor at bay by convincing them that they would receive their riches in the hereafter, rather than the here and now.

THE GIRL WHO SAID GOODBYE
FOR THE LAST TIME

Aaron recalled something he had once read:

Long-haired preachers come out every night,
Try to tell you what's wrong and what's right;
But when asked how 'bout something to eat
They will answer with voices so sweet:

You will eat, bye and bye,
In that glorious land above the sky;
Work and pray, live on hay,
You'll get pie in the sky when you die.

The starvation army they play,
They sing and they clap and they pray
'Till they get all your coin on the drum
Then they'll tell you when you're on the bum:

Holy Rollers and jumpers come out,
They holler, they jump and they shout.
Give your money to Jesus they say,
He will cure all diseases today.

If you fight hard for children and wife --
Try to get something good in this life --
You're a sinner and bad man, they tell,
When you die you will sure go to hell.

Workingmen of all countries, unite,
Side by side we for freedom will fight;
When the world and its wealth we have gained
To the grafters we'll sing this refrain:

J. Wayne Frye   227

THE GIRL WHO SAID GOODBYE
FOR THE LAST TIME

You will eat, bye and bye,
When you've learned how to cook and to fry.
Chop some wood, 'twill do you good,
And you'll eat in the sweet bye and bye.

Aaron was so distraught that he decided to rail against God and the stupidity of religion that kept people in bondage to the wealthy and powerful. "I tell you, you heaven's holy devil, you don't exist; but that, if you did, I would curse you so that your heaven would quiver with the fire of hell! I tell you, I have offered my service for the good of mankind, and you repulsed me; and I turn my back on you for all eternity, because you did not know compassion! I tell you that I am about to die of loneliness and misery, and yet I mock you and all you are supposed to stand for, because you are a hypocritical mockery of fairness in the world! You Heaven God with death staring me in the face--I tell you, I would rather rot in hell than bow before those who live in mansions in this abominable nation of whores who sell their souls for money. I am filled with contempt for your divine paltriness; and I choose the abyss of destruction for a perpetual slumber where I will at least be with those who spat in your eye and told you that your so-called religion was a farce of perpetual slavery that kept the wealthy in control while the truly kind and compassionate were cast into the fires of capitalistic damnation sanctioned by your representative here on earth."

THE GIRL WHO SAID GOODBYE
FOR THE LAST TIME

"I tell you your heaven, if it admits those who claim righteousness here on earth, is full of the most crass-headed idiots and poverty-stricken in spirit! I am the wrath of the devil of righteous indignation. I worship he who has pitchfork in hand rather than you, because I am the heavy sword of retribution that rains down upon those who trample upon dignity and fairness in an economic system that is a gross abomination."

As Aaron railed toward the heavens, people passed by with mild fascination that an old man would be standing in the snow railing against God, as they were all used to people praising the heavenly father rather than calling him out for mismanagement and gross negligence.

Exhausted from his mental breakdown, Aaron stood in the same spot, still whispering oaths and abusive epithets under his breath. He found another bench, cleared the snow and sat down. As he did so, in Minnie's apartment, there was a visitor asking her questions.

"So, just what did you tell Mr. Adams?"

Minnie, frightened but not bowing to her fear, replied, "What the hell business is it of yours? I owe you no explanations."

The visitor moved toward her with ill intent, and

she knew that the end was near. She spat in his face, as she said "fuck you and the horse you rode in on."

Those were her last words. She felt his hands tighten around her neck and she knew that struggling was useless. She simply let herself go limp and accepted her fate.

Aaron began to think of Lina, and how she had offered him the warmth of her body, but more importantly, the warmth of her soul. He needed help to overcome his descent back into madness that he had kept at bay for awhile. Yes, she could help him battle the demons that were now reclaiming him. He started toward her house, and as he passed by Minnie's on the way, he noticed that police cars were out front, lining the street. He walked over to a uniformed officer and said, "What's going on?"

"None of your business old man. Move on. Just move on."

Aaron, feeling that old brazenness when confronted with arrogance, said "I am a citizen of this city, and you work for me asshole. Don't tell me to move on with that kind of arrogance. Show me some respect. You are a servant of the people, and guess what, I, and other poor people like me are the people and we all are entitled to respect."

THE GIRL WHO SAID GOODBYE
FOR THE LAST TIME

"Listen old dude, don't fuck with New York's finest or you'll spend the night in the lock-up."

Just as he said that, Detective Brennan walked up. "Johnson, show this citizen a little respect. This is Aaron Adams. This fellow used to have a lot of juice in this town, before he became a Skid Row bum."

Aaron looked up at the slightly taller Brennan and said, "Well, if it isn't Mr. On-the-Take himself. How's the graft business this week Brennan?"

Brennan, very sternly replied "Adams, you played out in this town. I suggest you move on and forget about what is going on here."

"Brennan, is Minnie dead?"

"She is. You know anything about her death?"

"Yeah, I know that she had some information that was vital to a case I am working on. My guess is that the killer of Clarisse Coleman knew it too, and decided to snuff her."

Brennan, a look of disdain on his face, pointed his right index finger at Aaron. "Been a long time since we tangled Adams. Don't fuck with me. Who is your client?"

THE GIRL WHO SAID GOODBYE
FOR THE LAST TIME

"Privileged information asshole. Get a court writ and I may answer the question before a judge."

Brennan knew that legally he was stymied. "OK Aaron. You win this round. By the way, I thought you were dead. Nice to see you aren't. I still dream of bringing you down no matter how old and frail you are."

Laughing, Aaron replied "I'll never be too old to best you Brennan. If I go down, I'll take you with me."

Aaron walked up the street, but he was glancing back with his peripheral vision. He saw Brennan cross the street and walk over to a grey Mercedes, go to the back door as the window rolled down and lean in to talk to someone. The guy in the back seat had white hair.

Aaron's mind was once again descending into that dark pit of despair as he thought of his beloved Jasmine, even as he headed toward Lina Olman's place. He felt something swelling up inside him. There was a pain in his gut. Yes, it was that old feeling that all hell was about to break lose, and that Aaron would be right in the middle of it. Instincts die hard, and Aaron's instincts had been dormant for two years, but they had been resurrected by the mysterious woman in the black veil. Who the hell was she thought Aaron?

THE GIRL WHO SAID GOODBYE
FOR THE LAST TIME

Despite their age difference, Lina Olman had fallen deeply in love with Aaron Adams. Even though she knew he loved another woman, she saw in this incredible man a great depth of compassion for those who were marginalized by a society where all the good flowed to those at the top of the economic ladder. His kindness and devotion to justice made her love rise to the surface and float gently on a sea of blissful contentment in the arms of a man old enough to be her grandfather.

As Aaron stood in the doorway broadly smiling at her, she reached up and melted into his frail arms. She ushered him in and they spent the night talking and resting in the warmth of each others embrace.

The next morning they sat at the kitchen table discussing the woman in the veil. It was then that Lina said, "Aaron, you are a practical man. I know you look upon religion as a harbinger of evil that traps people in superstition and imprisons their minds in silliness, but take my word for it; there are things which simply defy explanation. Don't get me wrong, I know magicians have walked on water for years, even before Jesus did it. I know that the tales of Jesus were nothing but a recapitulation of prior tales from ancient texts. I know that even the flood and Noah were stories recounted long before the Bible, so I am an eternal sceptic who believes only what can be proved beyond a reasonable doubt. I don't see it with my own eyes, then I question it, but that does not mean that things don't exist in this world that defy explanation. You must remember that my dear."

Aaron reached over and placed his hand on hers. "Lina, I think I love you. I still love Jasmine, but I love you too. I am going to the 7/11 and get a paper. I want to see what is up with Minnie's murder. I'll be right back."

Little events in life irrevocably alter things for both good and bad. Aaron's decision to get a paper would save his life, but leaving her alone would cost Lina hers.

Yet though a man gets many wounds in his breast,
He dies not, until his appointed time.
The limit of his life span
is ticking on destiny's clock.
Nor does the man who by the hearth at home
sits still, escape the doom that fate decrees.
Aaron Adams' life had long ago been
Placed in the hands of the God of fate.
Nothing in heaven or earth could make him late.

Aaron was gone about ten minutes, and as he walked back to Lina's, he noticed an unmarked police car pull away from the curb in front of Lina's apartment. Brennan was in it.

THE GIRL WHO SAID GOODBYE
FOR THE LAST TIME

He got a sinking feeling in the pit of his stomach as he raced toward her apartment. The door was open and Lina was lying by the sofa with a bullet wound between her eyes. Only a small speck of blood slowly trickled out. Aaron did not have to feel her pulse. He had seen too many dead people in his life. Lina was gone. He kneeled beside her and sighed as he felt her hand one last time. She knew too much, but probably didn't even know what she knew that caused her death. Brennan had killed Minnie too in all likelihood or maybe it was the Chauffeur, but definitely not William Cardigan. He was the type man who ordered someone else to do his killing. But Aaron knew why they all had been killed. They had seen Cardigan with Clarisse. That was the connection, and Warren Cardigan had simply been the reason for Clarisse's murder. His father could not tolerate his offspring falling in love with a prostitute. His haughty arrogance would not permit that. She was not good enough to bear the Cardigan name. It was too special.

Aaron looked around the room for something he could use for a weapon. He was going to kill three people. He would not depend on justice to play out, because with people like Cardigan there was no justice. He would hire some high priced attorneys and walk. How ionic he thought that in a country where you had to get a licence to drive, but needed no such formality to procure a gun, he, for the first time in his life, was ready to go into battle without a weapon.

He noticed that Clarisse's purse was on the coffee table. He walked over, opened it and removed two credit cards. He had his weapons.

He went into the bedroom, removed the sheet from the bed and placed it over Lina's body. He walked out the door into the bright morning sunlight, but vowed that darkness would fall on a killer.

THE GIRL WHO SAID GOODBYE
FOR THE LAST TIME

CHAPTER 12
AND DIE WITH REAL PEOPLE

Aaron was going to find Brennan in a quiet place away from the crowd and kill him. Aaron had killed before, but premeditation was a rarity. Yet, this time he felt no remorse in planning the end of a man who had no compassion and no core to him. Brennan had solicitous contempt for anything that stood between him and the accumulation of money. He was the very worst in a cop – one who saw his position as nothing more than a licence to serve the rich and powerful in order to accumulate riches for himself at the expense of those on the lower rungs of the socio-economic ladder who had no one to champion their cause. The oath said "to protect and serve" but there should be something added – "to protect and serve the moneyed class at all costs." The police, the politicians had long ago abrogated responsibility to reach down with the hand of compassion and protect the poor from the predator class that owned the government and made sure that the police served their real purpose – to protect those at the top from people who might demand a fair distribution of income. Ask yourself, thought Aaron, how long it takes for the police to respond to a call from the ghetto compared to a call from a Park Avenue penthouse. That was illustrative of where the real priorities lay. Well, there were a few good ones, but the bad ones were simply too powerful for the good ones to tackle. Those who still cared were just gobbled up and discarded by a system that tolerated no dissent.

Aaron was about to eliminate one of the bad ones. He waited outside the 33rd Precinct for Brennan. His heart raced with anticipation. He was an old man now, and if he gave Brennan an edge, it would be the end for Aaron. Hell, he was at the end anyway, but he had two others he had to kill before he made his final exit, and he wanted to make sure Brennan paid the supreme price for killing such a wonderful woman. To him, she was scum, but Aaron knew who the real scum was. It was Brennan and all those like him who served the interests of those at the top. Aaron was the last of a dying breed, the last of those who refused to cower in fear before the high and mighty. He was the avenging angel who swung the sword of retribution for those who had no one to fight for them anymore. He smiled and prepared for the one thing that made his life worthwhile. He had the balls to tackle the authorities, those who felt exalted and privileged. He smiled.

He stood across the street from the precinct and watched as Brennan came out with a colleague, waved goodbye to him and headed toward his co-op on Fifth Avenue. He made about $100,000 a year for a job that was worth maybe $70,000 tops, but the police in the big cities were part of the privileged class and were grossly overpaid, because they were the last line of defence between the poor and the rich. They had to be well-paid in order to keep them from going over to the enemy – the poor.

Aaron followed at a reasonable distance to avoid detection, and when Brennan got to the building with its marble columns out front and its glistening façade that smacked of exclusivity, he almost laughed out loud wondering why the Police Commissioner didn't ask how a man making $100,000 a year could afford to live in a co-op building where the apartments started at 3.2 million. Maybe because the grossly overpaid Police Commissioner was, himself, living in a co-op on Park Avenue where the prices started at a little over 5 million. Welcome to the world of the modern "public servant" where the phrase public servant meant that the public you were serving first and foremost was yourself. Government service, at one time, was a calling that attracted those who wanted to help. Not any more.

No doubt, Brennan was enjoying a lunch prepared by a Hispanic maid from Mexico or some other poor Central American country, who had to go home to the ghetto after cleaning and serving the people in the high rise condos in upper Manhattan.

THE GIRL WHO SAID GOODBYE
FOR THE LAST TIME

Aaron waited patiently for almost an hour and then Brennan came out of the apartment, strolled out to a waiting car and he and the driver pulled away. Aaron hailed a cab and got the customary curious look when he said, "follow that car."

Fortunately, Aaron had the money given him by Warren Cardigan, so he wasn't worried about the bill as they made their way for what seemed about 30 minutes to lower Manhattan, which was out of Brennan's jurisdiction. "Out for some lower Manhattan graft," whispered Aaron to himself.

Sure enough, they stopped in front of a dive bar and Brennan got out and waved the driver away. Aaron paid the cabby and walked to the front of the bar, looked in the window and saw Brennan conversing with someone who looked like a punk who probably dealt drugs. He was really nervous, bouncing up and down as he chewed gum. Brennan motioned toward the back of the bar and they walked to the exit where Brennan slowly pushed open the door and waited for the guy to walk into the back alley. Aaron walked around behind the building and stood by the side of the alleyway as he listened to the conversation between the two.

"I tell you Brennan that I ain't holding out. Times is real bad. Come on. You know I got more sense than to stiff you. I got you the thousand extra but you expect too much. Two thousand more a month is cutting deep into my profits. I ain't no big time pusher, just a little guy trying to make a buck. The kids over at PS 345 ain't got rich parents like those people who live up town, man. I ain't a high level pusher who caters to kids with parents who work uptown. You know my limitations. I got to work for nickels and dimes. Come on now."

Brennan leaned in real close. "Porky, we all got problems, me included. The deal is that protection just got more expensive. I got some beat cops I have to pay off too. We all got families. Things are tough all over. It is two thousand more a month now."

Aaron moved slowly into the back alley, but Brennan's instincts were sharp. He turned quickly and had his rod out before Aaron was more than ten feet away. He shoved Porky onto the ground and he fell face up about five feet from Aaron. All the advantage belonged to Brennan and Aaron knew it. Aaron looked down at Porky and said, "Don't move punk."

Porky was shaking like a high rise in downtown LA during an earthquake along the San Andreas Fault. He managed to mutter, "Ain't moving man. Ain't moving. You dudes is in total control here. Total."

THE GIRL WHO SAID GOODBYE
FOR THE LAST TIME

His gun levelled at Aaron, Brennan let a sinister smile creep across his face. "Listen old dude. You figured out it was me iced Minnie and that whore, uh. Good thing you were gone or you'd been iced right along with that cock sucking bitch you were humping. You are a dirty old man Aaron. Yeah, a dirty old man. Bet that bitch really got that old wrinkled pecker of yours hard didn't she. If I'd had time I would have humped her good before I pulled the trigger. Now, before I send you off to that old private eye home in the sweet bye and bye I suppose a detective like you would like to know all the details. Simple, I saw Cardigan's name in the trick book and simply decided to help out a rich dude who might help me out for doing him a good turn. Went right to the old man instead of the son, because you always know the old man is the brains in these situations, and I figured it out easy like. He picks up Clarisse one night and offers her some big bucks to leave his son alone. She is in love, so she turns down William Cardigan. Cardigan sends his chauffeur over to dispatch her, because rich guys never do their own dirty work. OK, I tell Cardigan, she was just a low-life whore, no big deal. Then when Minnie and Lina enter the picture I take care of them for him – extra charge of course. End of story once I take you out. That takes care of all lose ends."

Porky had managed to get to his knees and got on all fours preparing to make a dash for it, which gave Aaron cover for a brief second. He reached in his pocket and pulled out one of the credit cards just as Porky took four bullets in the back meant for Aaron. As Porky fell to the ground, Brennan squeezed off the last two rounds in the gun. It didn't even hurt Aaron thought, feeling only a slight sting as the bullets entered his left side. The credit card sliced Brennan's jugular as Aaron whipped it across his neck and Brennan fell to the ground trying to stem the flow of blood. Aaron looked down and smiled at him, "Not going to happen Brennan, even if you could call the paramedics, you would be dead before you finished the call. Adios."

No need to take the gun thought Aaron as he knew that Brennan had already expended six shells. Anyway, the credit card was a damn good weapon. He tossed the card he used to kill Brennan on the ground beside him so the authorities could connect him to the murder of Lina Olman. Hell, they would probably cover it up and make Brennan some kind of hero who took on a drug dealer in a back alley. New York's finest going down in a blaze of glory defending the poor youth. Yeah, that's the way they would play it alright.

The lady at the reception desk recognized Aaron and buzzed him right up to Warren's office. Warren Cardigan seemed surprised to see Aaron, but very courteously asked him in. "So, how is the investigation going?"

"Well, one of the culprits is dead, laying in an alley in lower Manhattan. I believe you know Detective Brennan. His days of hassling and railroading the innocent are over."

There was a large box on Warren's desk. Aaron wondered what was in it. He continued the conversation. "Seems Brennan was working for your father, trying to clean up a rather sloppy mess."

Warren, a serious look on his drawn face, said "Yes, I know Mr. Adams. My father is the one responsible for Clarisse's demise. He as good as admitted it to me this morning when I confronted him. Of course he says it was my fault."

Aaron noticed Warren's hand moving slowly toward the box on the desk. Beside the box was an old style wool Fedora hat, the kind that men wore maybe 50 years ago. Was he planning on going out in the winter cold? Nice hat thought Aaron; it would keep the wet snow off his head. "So, you know that I am going to have to bring your father and his chauffeur to justice."

"Good luck Mr. Adams. It will not be an easy task. You have never gone up against anyone as ruthless as my father. I assure you." He was now actually fondling the top of the open box.

"I can be pretty ruthless myself."

Warren looked down at the blood that was now dripping on the floor from Aaron's wound. "You are hurt Mr. Adams. You should get to a doctor."

"It is way too late Warren, too late in so many ways."

Warren had his hand inside the box. "It is too late for me too Mr. Adams. I am a big disappointment to my father, but I am a bigger disappointment to myself. I should have left and immediately run away with Clarisse. She would be alive today if I had been more forceful. If had a backbone; if I had stood up to my father."

Aaron knew what was in the box on Warren's desk. He jumped up and shouted "no" just as Warren took out the gun. Warren looked him directly in the eyes and said, "It is the only way I can be with Clarisse," as he put the barrel to his temple, pulled the trigger and brain fragments splattered against the far wall.

There was a great commotion as people came running into the office. The screams, the hysteria were sufficient for Aaron to simply turn unnoticed and walk away. He never looked back. There was no need to do so. Warren Cardigan was free now, free of his father and free of the pain he had endured without Clarisse. He was wrong though about being with her thought Aaron. Death was the end. After that there was nothing else, absolutely nothing. Aaron would be free soon, too, but first he had to make certain William Cardigan faced justice.

A life can be like a star, a living fire to lighten the darkness, leading out into the expansion of hope. Aaron had lost hope when Jasmine left him. He had found a bit of hope in the arms of Lina, but like most things in life, just when you think all those stars are in perfect alignment something catastrophic happens and the darkness prevails. Aaron had hoped that Warren would take some solace in finding out the truth, but like Aaron, he had lost hope.

Hope was gone from Aaron's life and the society of greed had hijacked hope for everyone but the few. Aaron always hoped that there were aliens somewhere out there in the vast cosmos, because the thought of humans being the best there was made him cringe with fear. If humans were the best the universe had to offer, the universe was in big trouble. Yet, there were the few who seemed to give humanity hope – people like Clarisse, Lina and Warren.

THE GIRL WHO SAID GOODBYE
FOR THE LAST TIME

Aaron had always said that the universe was full of intelligent life, since obviously it was too intelligent to come to earth, because earth was filled with people who simply acquiesced to their own slavery by lining up for their chains.

Well, Aaron had never had any chains binding him. He had always refused to play the game others played. He had never been afraid of the William Cardigans of the world, and he was about to go out in a blaze of glory taking down the high and mighty one last time.

There are times when all the stars simply seem to align perfectly in our lives. As Aaron stepped out of the revolving doors from the Cardigan Towers, he realized this was one of those times for him. Yes, everything was falling into place perfectly when it came to meting out justice for Clarisse.

As he walked down the steps toward the street, the chauffeur was opening the door for William Cardigan. Cardigan saw Aaron and quickly told the chauffeur, "Nail that son-of-a-bitch, now."

The chauffeur started to reach inside his pocket for a gun, but before he could pull it, Aaron had the other credit card out and with a swift slash across the neck, the chauffeur crumbled to the pavement in a heap, desperately trying to stem the flow of blood. He was dead, but just didn't know it.

Cardigan desperately tried to retreat back into the car, but Aaron leaned forward and said, "I am your judge, jury and executioner asshole. Your money won't save you from me." He raised the credit card and swiftly brought it across his neck and in a quiet whisper said, "Catch you in hell asshole, and when I see you I'll shove a pitch fork up your ass."

Cardigan's money didn't save him from the wrath of Aaron Adams. He died like a whimpering baby, trying to keep the blood from flowing out of the huge gash in his neck. It was a futile effort.

It had all happened so fast no one had even seen it. Aaron simply walked down the street and tossed the credit card into a water fountain. He laughed and whispered to himself, "Charge up some justice and send the bill to William Cardigan's estate."

He grabbed his side and felt the gapping hole that was allowing his life to gradually seep away with each drop. He didn't want to die in uptown Manhattan with the rich assholes who ruled the city. He wanted to get back to his dingy hotel in the ghetto and die with real people.

THE GIRL WHO SAID GOODBYE
FOR THE LAST TIME

CHAPTER 13
IN ITS RADIANT WARMTH

Death leaves a heartache no one can heal,
Love leaves a memory no one can steal.
Life is eternal, and love is immortal.
Death is only a horizon with an open portal.
Now together forever in eternal bliss,
Two lovers arise from the abyss.

In her eternal sleep she saw the skies of red
From the zenith to her lover's fevered lips,
And all the dark tide blushed with blazing tips.
Her burning heart fierce flames suddenly shed,
Each like a snake lifting its crested head,
Sprang they like from some dull eclipse.

Shadowed stars suckled heaven's sweet tips.
Weltering in wretched fog, she oozed and bled.
Heaven, sea, and earth in wild confusion burned,
And by that light she cried for help from one
Who was ablaze with pain but still shined bright,
So that he would lead her to the light.

Despite the fact he felt his life slowly ebbing away, Aaron was happy. He had solved one last case and brought the murderers of Clarisse to justice.

Darkness began to descend on the city and he knew that it was also descending on the life of

THE GIRL WHO SAID GOODBYE
FOR THE LAST TIME

Aaron Adams. He would die without his beloved Jasmine by his side, but he had found Lina and she had made his spirits soar, made him feel like a man one last time. His life had been good for the most part, because he had been able to help so many people. Yeah, he thought, able to help everyone but myself.

When we see death reaching out its boney fingers beckoning us, our thoughts are a kalidiocopic cacophony of what we have done and what we have left undone. The attraction of sex is so powerful that it pervades even our final thoughts as we head down that dark river of no return. Aaron, struggling to keep his feet moving forward, recalled one of his earliest sexual escapades with a young girl as they sat in the living room of her home. Her parents were in the next room, so the two teenagers had to be very careful about what they did. Still, young lovers seeking sexual excitement cannot be deterred. She had fondled Aaron though his pants, causing a cataclysmic explosion of passion that soiled his underwear. Ah, his adolescence had been filled with such events.

Then there was the girl, he couldn't even remember her name, who sat in front of him in English class. She placed her spiral binder notebook on her side, leaned on it and tilted it upward hiding her left breast from the teacher so that Aaron could put his hand on it and playful massage it. That, too, had made him explode in his pants. It was a daily occurrence that certainly made English his favourite subject.

Those events were almost 70 years ago, but Aaron recalled them all as if they were yesterday's occurrences that still shined brightly in his mind. Then he reflected on his twenty years with Jasmine and the tears started to flow.

When he got to the corner of the Subway entrance on 43rd Place, the street commenced suddenly to swim around before his eyes; it buzzed vacantly in his head, and he staggered up against the wall of a building. He was close to the hotel, but he could simply go no farther. As he fell up against the building, he remained barely standing, and he felt his consciousness slowly ebbing away. He lifted his right foot and tried to start walking, but could not move. His strength had simply dissipated. He did not want to die on the street. He had to find the energy to move.

He clenched his teeth, wrinkled his brow, and rolled his eyes in a desperate attempt to remain conscious. It was clear to him that he was about to die. He stretched out his hands, and pushed himself back from the wall. The street danced wildly around him. He began to cough up blood. He vowed to himself not to die standing there.

THE GIRL WHO SAID GOODBYE
FOR THE LAST TIME

The darkness seemed to completely surround him except for a tiny light in the distance. Time edged slowly forward. He let himself sink down on the pavement, just sitting in the wet snow, but still there was that faint light in the distance. The light was obscured by a fog that was slowly forming around it, making it blurry and only slightly discernable.

The light in the dense fog was about fifteen feet above the sidewalk, seeming to almost float in the darkness. He had an overpowering urge to get to that light. He suddenly felt as light as a feather, almost like he could float the 50 metres to the light.

He seemed to float toward the light. His feet were moving, but they were as light as a feather. He heard the clock in the nearby All Saviours Catholic Church strike nine times. Again he sank under the weight of his prolonged agony over the wound in his side. The hollow whirring in his head made him so dizzy that the light ahead seemed to be undulating.

He stared straight ahead, kept his eyes fixed on the light glimmering in the fog. It seemed to be beckoning him now, calling out to him. It was as if it offered a warmth, solace from the pain and agony that had embraced him most of his life. He had to get to the light.

J. Wayne Frye

THE GIRL WHO SAID GOODBYE
FOR THE LAST TIME

He dragged himself ever forward, until the light became more visible. He knew the light. Yes, it was the lamppost where the black veiled lady had met him many times. There she stood in her veil, her arms outstretched as if wanting to embrace him. Aaron moved toward her and nearly fell into her arms. She whispered softly to him, "My dear Aaron, you have brought my lover back to me. It was not he who killed me. I can now move from purgatory into the bright light of hope that awaits us. You Aaron Adams have made this possible."

Aaron could not believe that it was Clarisse who was the mysterious woman in the veil. He simply did not believe in ghosts. Yet, one was fondly embracing him.

She raised the long black veil, and an incredibly, magnificently beautiful woman gazed into his eyes and said, "You, Aaron Adams, are a fine and decent man, and I tell you that your mental anxious is about to end. That which you want above all else awaits you at your hotel. Go my dear man and meet your destiny, and I sincerely thank you for ending my misery.

She turned and walked toward the alley where Aaron had accompanied her once before. As she got to the alley entrance, a tall man wearing a Fedora hat stepped out from the darkness, took her hand and the two of them walked into the alley as a bright light seemed to bathe them in its radiant warmth.

THE GIRL WHO SAID GOODBYE
FOR THE LAST TIME

EPILOGUE
LOVE JASMINE

Light seemed to never shine
In a misty field of horrific pain.
The world for him was
A door that was bolted,
And the lock would never
Slide to open into hope.

His was a harsh journey
Down a tunnel of despair.
The edges of sanity were
But smudges on a wall
Filled with the mosaics
Drawn by his lost soul.

The air was so thick
That breath came harshly.
Moving toward distant light
Still offered no hope.
Everything was solemnly set
In eternal, perfect blackness.

Life is a ponderous journey for most people. Yes, happiness often abounds, but the sadness endured can sometimes be so overwhelming that we actually long for that final exit from what is often referred to as the veil of tears. Aaron had observed what appeared to be the ghosts of

THE GIRL WHO SAID GOODBYE
FOR THE LAST TIME

Clarisse and Warren walk hand-in-hand into a blissful eternity. Oh, how he wished it were true, wished that there could be eternal blissfulness for those who had endured so much heartache in life. Still, he could not imagine a blissful eternity for himself. Maybe that was too much to expect. As he reached down and tried to stem the flow of blood, all he wanted was the peacefulness, the serenity, the finality of death. He was just a tired old man who had endured all he could. He wanted it to all be over.

He knew he might not make it up the three flights of stairs to his room, but, as always, the elevator was out of order, so he had no choice but to try and climb the stairs. He struggled up each flight until he stood in the corridor of the third floor, looking down the hallway where his room seemed like a journey of a thousand kilometres, but he wanted to lie down, lie down and die in bed thinking of his beloved Jasmine.

There was no pain from his wound now, only the recognition that the end was finally near. He noticed his door was open as the light from his room filtered into the dimly lit corridor. Who was in his room? Yeah, probably his roommate had just left the door open. Yet, there was a distinct brightness to the light, almost as if it was giving off an angelic glow. He sighed and thought maybe God had sent the Angel of Light to carry me to my home with Jesus. Then, he laughed out loud at the ridiculousness of the thought, as he leaned on the wall and pushed himself forward with his right hand toward his door.

The laughter had disturbed the two men standing by the pay phone at the end of the hallway. However, it had also alerted the person in his room to the fact that Aaron was in the corridor, because the person recognized the laugh. She had gotten up from the chair beside Aaron's bed and ran to the doorway. She stood there within five feet of Aaron just staring at him. Aaron could not believe his eyes. It was the Angel of Light. Yes, from heaven on high the Angel of Light had been sent to embrace him in his last hour. It was Jasmine!

He fell forward into her arms. As she caught his frail body she looked toward the two men and shouted, "Call 911!"

She managed to help him into the room and gently guide him into his bed. The blood was flowing profusely now and Aaron could not talk. All he could do was stare at the loveliest woman he had ever seen.

The bright lights outside the dingy hotel room window flashed a neon beacon of lost promise for those who had finally descended to the bottom of despair on a street of broken dreams. The beautiful Jasmine Alexander whispered to him, "Finally, finally I have found you my love."

Aaron struggled for words and in a faint voice he said, "Why did you leave me? I could have gotten well. I know I could have licked my illness."

A puzzled look on her face, Jasmine said, "Leave you? What are you talking about? You left me."

Aaron quizzically replied, "The envelope. You left the envelope."

Jasmine, now thoroughly confused, said, "Did you not read the note?"

Aaron, barely able to raise his right hand, pointed to his left breast coat pocket. Jasmine gently removed the envelope and said, as she tore it open and removed the note, "You ninny. Aaron, you never even read it."

Aaron, now tears in his eyes, as she unfolded the note, said "I could not bear to read your goodbye. It was too much for me, too much."

She held the note up before his eyes, and Aaron read it for the first time:

THE GIRL WHO SAID GOODBYE
FOR THE LAST TIME

AARON, I AM SPENDING THE NIGHT AT TRUDY'S. YOUR DINNER IS IN THE MICROWAVE. I WILL SEE YOU IN THE MORNING MY DEAR.

LOVE,

JASMINE